CRUEL PROVIDENCE

By

Marie Jean Davis

Cruel Providence

Cruel Providence – by Marie Jean Davis

With love and happiness I dedicated this book to my three daughters, Connie, Shellie and Shannon and to my son, Trenton. Without them I would not be the person that I am. Thank you for allowing me to be part of your ever-evolving lives.

Chapter 1

In rural England in the late 1700s, Miss Katherin Hampton was enchanted with her life in a home filled with joy and affection from her two loving parents and four siblings. She enjoyed a good life with her family. Being the eldest, she prided herself in the motherly instincts and affection that she bestowed as though she were raising her three sisters and one brother alone. They all looked up to Katherin for her charitable nature, good disposition, and above all her extremely loving countenance. The children took to heart the direction Katherin eagerly instilled in them, and she was pleased with their reciprocal temperament.

Katherin's Papa was quick to mention her natural endowment to motherhood brought on by good upbringing from parents, who by all accounts, adored their children. For over eighteen years, the family had been blessed with wealth. They, of course, had many servants such as a governess, a cook, maids, and a butler who were gentle and loving, as the family would not allow for anyone less than caring into their home. Katherin's mother, Constance Hampton was of royal bloodline, and thus expected to enjoy the finest things in life.

Mr. Edward Hampton, for his part, was admired in the business world for his shrewd and intelligent nature. He had the ability to attract many fine business ventures simply by word of mouth. He could turn any enterprise into a success story. Therefore, the opportunities were limitless, as his reputation preceded him everywhere he went. Although, he was a loving father, he also spent countless hours away due to his occupation.

Due to Mr. Hampton's ever demanding work, raising the children was left in the capable hands of Mrs. Constance Hampton. Constance was a tall and slender woman who had kept her elegant figure even after giving birth to five children. Fine boned, with a very pleasant face adorned of rosy, thin lips, and hair that was stylishly coiffed in the latest fashion, she was unusually pale and suffered from the sun should she remain outdoors too long. Constance was delicate but had a regal appearance. She was a perfectionist if you could ever imagine one to be. It all stemmed from her strict upbringing among her royal relations who prided themselves in their manners, and calm emotional temperament. The aristocratic family was constantly on display, and society looked up to them for the role model they portrayed. However proper her upbringing had been, Constance had lots of love for her five beautiful children, in turn helping them to reach their potential. The eldest was Katherin, followed by Margaret, Genevieve, Jane and the youngest not yet seven, Edward. He had been, as you might say, spoiled since he was the last-born of the family. Constance had gone through five rather difficult births before Edward III finally deigned to make his appearance. Mrs. Hampton was absolutely delighted. Finally, a son had been born in their midst. Constance was obviously grateful for being able to give her husband a son at long last. He was, of course, overjoyed with his son's arrival. While growing up among four sisters who showered him with affection, along with two doting parents, Edward could bring mayhem if not carefully supervised. He was a bright boy who enjoyed playtime, but for most of the time was very loving toward his siblings.

The parents worried if the worst were to happen to them before young Edward reached maturity, what would become of the children? The girls could not inherit the family's fortune, and young Edward was much too young to take on such a responsibility? The parents' absence would be a terrible burden on the children. In fact, this bothered the parents to the point that they both came up with an arrangement. A plan was necessary to ensure the preservation of the family's fortune, and of the legacy in the event of the parents' untimely demise.

It was now late winter in England. The sun was setting later in the night sky. And with the thawing of the last snow, vibrant, colourful spring flowers emerged from the dark loam as far as the eye could see. The fluffy clouds passing by on a bright sunny day gave the illusion of floating elegantly by the soft blue sky with slow graceful movements swirling about in the heavens. The crocuses, daffodils, and tulips adorned the landscape around the grounds of the estate. The spring was also the most refreshing season where everything burst forth with life, giving rise to spectacular moments indeed. The tree buds were having their own debut, which was a spectacular display of colours, and the thriving greenery was breathtaking. This time of year was the time where not only plants were coming to life, but also the inhabitants were rising out of their slumber that ensued during the course of the long winter months. The air was filled with the music of new birth and birds heralding the arrival of new life.

Katherin had blossomed from her childhood appearance to one of a young woman. She emerged out this past winter to a fine graceful young lady. She was growing more beautiful with each passing day. The golden shimmers of her blond hair only accentuated the ivory shades of her silken skin. It seemed to reflect the shades of roses in her cheeks and the softness of pearls over her hands. Katherin's bosom was now fuller and her entire body seemed to be more curvaceous and attractive. Her graceful mannerism would send shockwaves to any man, who would have been privileged enough to see her in her natural splendour. She kept close to home much of the time in fear that someone should take her away whether for marriage, or possibly steal her away like so many young women were of late. They all but disappeared without a trace, and were most likely sold, as articles would be at auctions, while others were transported to the Americas for good breeding stock, and sold at a mercantile like rolls of fabric.

The Hampton's were not going to see their beautiful princesses taken away and sold like cattle. Therefore, they had kept a tight rein on their daughters; their eldest in particular. She could perhaps someday save the family from impending doom should something happen to her parents before young Edward grew to a man.

This had brought some strain between the parents however, for Mrs. Hampton did not always agree with the business-minded man her husband had become. Of late, Mr. Hampton had become quite intense on securing their immediate financial future. Mrs. Hampton trusted that he would, and had made the right decision in order to keep his family with his fortune from getting in the wrong hands, or worse yet, taken by the government for taxes owed. In Constance's eyes, she did not believe that her husband could make a wrong decision, as he had proven over and over again to bring riches to the family fortune in excess then what they currently required.

Mr. Hampton himself came from a good family. He was the eldest of two boys born to his parents, Isabella and Edward Senior. They owned properties and wealth acquired through business ventures or through inheritance. Constance would not, and could not have married Mr. Hampton should his family being unable to prove his worth and his respectful ancestry.

Mr. Edward Hampton II was responsible for caring for his elderly parents, Isabella and Edward, who seem to have gone quite insane in their later years. The younger brother, Randal was a captain in the military and played no part in caring for the parents. While on military duties, Randal had gone missing while fighting enemies in some far away land. It had been almost five years since the family had heard news from the young man. He was by all accounts "presumed dead". The death of Edward's only brother had brought great sorrow to the family, who loved him. Edward in particular admired his younger brother, and had desperately tried to persuade him to partner with him in the business sector. However, Randal had not wanted to be working in the shadows of his older brother. He felt it wasn't his destiny. Randal had wanted to make his own mark in life than be called his brother's servant for this is all he would have become. Therefore, it was off to war. He had risen to the ranks of captain in a very short time for he possessed a bright mind and fortitude, which he seemed to have inherited as a family trait. Randal had been tall and lean with the strength that inspired respect from his troops.

He had been, by far, the more handsome of the two brothers. Edward Hampton, on the other hand, was a short man with dark brown hair but with a pleasant face that gave a more distinguished look than that of his younger brother.

Edward had grieved when his brother Randal left for the war. However, upon receiving word from Randal, mentioning how happy he was with his new appointment, Edward felt encouraged that his brother had made the right decision. Edward would receive letters from his brother somewhat regularly and had been very excited upon each of their arrivals. He would at once bring the letters home to read to the children in front of the fireplace.

Father would read the letters with such excitement and pleasure that it soon contaminated the entire household with pleasant and enjoyable thoughts. Uncle Randal had a talent to write where every sentence danced with life. He wrote about the strange people he encountered through his many travels abroad, not to mention the diverse array of animals he found in nature. Uncle Randal had such a way of bringing the beauty of nature to life that the Hampton family could visualize him and his surrounding in their minds while imagining being alongside their uncle, keeping the family closer together.

However once the letters had ceased to arrive, Father became quite despondent, and found it difficult to concentrate on work. After the news arrived of Randal being missing in action, Father fell quite ill at heart. He seemed to have lost interest in every matter that once brought him joy. Father then caught the influenza, and other ailments that he had never contracted before. It was in the fourth year of Uncle Randal's disappearance that Father had brought home a sickness that took hold of the entire family. It also caused the death of Mummy, and of little Maggie, for which Father blamed himself. Subsequently, the family heard news of Father's parents falling very ill. They soon passed away, further affecting Father's disposition to work and where his health suffered immensely.

After lying to rest so many members of his family, Father cried a great deal of the time. He grieved so that it was difficult to console him. Mummy's parents had come by to help; however they too found they were unable to restore Papa's good humour or disposition. Grandfather and Grandmamma had left after several weeks of futile efforts to bring Papa out of his depression, without appeasing him in the slightest. Unfortunately, through this sad time, Father had lost quite a lot of the family fortune, where he wasn't able to continue to bring prosperity to his family, something he once accomplished with little effort.

The time came when he would have to secure the family's wealth again, as he had promised his dying wife, Constance. Mummy had made Father promise to do whatever it took to secure the family's wealth, ensuring the girls were looked after, while young Edward III would grow into a young man. He could then take over the family affairs. Father had promised to do his duty, and so he must.

Katherin believed that it was unfair not to allow the females in the family to inherit their property and assets, if something should happen to her Papa.

Thus, in the end, their father had made all the necessary arrangements to ensure the children's future. Now that it was spring, and as nature came to life, so did Papa's promise to his dying wife.

Of course Katherin was coming of age and her debut were only several weeks away. Mr. Hampton had already set in motion the events that were to follow.

Her father had called Katherin into the parlour where he sat her down for a discussion. He went on to describe the night of Katherin's debut, which she was already dreaming of attending. Katherin was pleased to be at long last attending her own unveiling. She would finally have some excitement after many long months of hardship, with the mourning of her beloved sister and her Mummy. The Hampton family wore black for many months afterwards, as the customary dress were black during a full year after the passing of any family member. And with the passing of so many for such a long time, it appeared that they would never again don colour garments. As though the spring air had brought the glorious colours back to life, so did a grand ball bring promises of undreamt pleasures the family had not enjoyed during the bereavement.

Katherin hoped it would not only be her coming out into society, but would also provide her Papa with a diversion to mend his broken heart. Katherin had for countless nights laid awake concerned with her father's health. She did not want her Papa to fall ill as her grandparents had fallen ill, for shortly thereafter followed the sickness of the mind. With the family still grieving over Randal's death, Katherin felt that another setback would only result in tragedy of the worst kind.

Now Papa wanted to have a discussion regarding the arrangements that were made.

"Yes, Papa," Katherin went on with excitement in her voice.

"Presently, you are going to the ball, and of course, I expect you to be on your best behaviour. There will be many influential aristocratic gentlemen who can provide you with all the fineries and the desirable life style that you would ever need and are accustomed to. Your dear Mummy wanted you to have the finest life could afford," he explained to her.

"Yes, Papa, I wish to please you, and I am extremely excited. I cannot contain myself. I will do what is expected of me, of course, and whatever is necessary to ensure your happiness. Was there other matters of concern to you that you wished to discuss, Papa?"

"No, not at the moment, dear one," he replied, not wanting to take away his eldest girl's enjoyment. He therefore kept quiet and did not add undo strain to what was seemingly the happiest days of his beautiful daughter's life.

"I'll come up to read the night's tale to the children. Simply help prepare the children for bed, my darling," he asked Katherin before she closed the door behind her.

Chapter 2

Katherin's debut into society was but a few days away. Yet there were many preparations to be made. Miss Louise, their governess was fussing over the way a young lady should hold herself in public. She wanted young Katherin to have an impeccable stance. Miss Louise was overly concerned with matters of Katherin's posture. Katherin was not the perfection that her governess desired, although she was dedicated, and appreciated her role along with her position within the family. Miss Louise was also concerned how this would reflect on her skills as a governess. She was an austere woman with hair drawn into a chignon at the nape of her neck, and wire-rimmed glasses sitting on the edge of her pert nose. Her thinned lips seldom smiled, although she did when the children pleased her. Her small frame belied her strength and she was impeccably dressed each day she taught the children in manners and daily lessons.

The recent lessons had put undue stress on Katherin's sense of duty and while not wanting to upset Miss Louise, Katherin attempted to comply with her pomp and decorum instructions. Nonetheless, Katherin found it terribly upsetting that she was not the perfection her mother would have expected her to be. On the other hand, Constance had such aplomb and such manners and posture; it would have brought a man to his knees from the sheer elegance that she evoked. Her portrayal of the true feminine depiction was done with such ease, although elegance and grace was the only descriptive words of Constance's demeanour. She had the sophistication

13

and allure born out of good breeding. Katherin feared she could not bring happiness to her Papa, if she didn't reflect her mother's posture and attitude. She practiced relentlessly with each passing day, for what appeared weeks on end, while the unmoving governess would not be satisfied.

According to Katherin, Miss Louise must have been educated under a constant cloud of dissatisfaction with every outcome, rather than encouragement. Katherin feared she was hopelessly flawed, and would bring shame to her family should she not perfect this seemingly non-problematic task. However flawed she might have been, Katherin possessed the beauty that was bestowed upon her from her mother's side of the family. Then again her mother had allowed her children to have less than perfect poise for fear that she may turn into a dreadful mother, who would insist on more perfection from her children than what was humanly possible. Instead, Constance wanted her children to be good at heart with a loving disposition, rather than be excessively preoccupied with other issues, which didn't matter as much. Then again the governess would have wished for additional hours in providing the necessary poise which society demanded of Katherin's debut.

Katherin had been especially dutiful with respect to her dance lessons, as well as the many other classes, which she felt were terribly exhaustive at the end of each day. She was tired to the point where sleep came quickly from the moment she slipped under the cover. She would start to dream immediately. Katherin had many dreams pertaining to the debutantes' ball, but one dream in particular had not gone according to what she would have wanted. She came to the conclusion that perhaps she was not meant to attend such an elaborate society function without first attending a smaller gathering. Yet, with the debutantes' ball two fortnights away, there would not be sufficient time for an utterly unimportant social event. Katherin sighed with resigned hopelessness that she may indeed disappoint her Papa. In the end however, she decided to approach her governess to assist in this rather trivial issue of attending a small social gathering, where she hoped to learn from observing others who probably had more refined manners than she did.

The next morning her governess entered Katherin's room. Katherin sat pondering the matter, giving her the opportune moment to seek her governess's opinion. Although, she would have preferred to speak with her own mother, Katherin was resigned to the fact that Miss Louise would be her only choice of confidante.

"May I speak with you in regards to my apprehension of the upcoming debut?" Katherin tried appealing to the governess's tender side with enormous hopes of obtaining plausible answers.

"Why, indeed you may, child," Miss Louise replied, only too pleased that Katherin finally reached out for what she presumed was the missing link to her becoming the perfect pupil.

"I have been practicing the social graces and posture as you directed. Yet, I have not felt satisfied with my efforts. I feel that it would be of great benefit to attend a social event that may provide a precursor to my presentation into society?"

"I may not be able to provide you with such a gathering with so little notice, my dear one," Miss Louise replied. Nevertheless, seeing the disappointment in Katherin's eyes, Miss Louise felt compelled, at the very least, to attempt to help her. "I do know of such a soirée in a few evenings from this day, then again I may not be able to provide you with an invitation with our time constraints. I will do what is possible in such a short notice, and will bring you news directly."

"Thank you for being so understanding, Miss Louise," Katherin said with such emotion that any governess would find difficult not to make a sincere attempt to please.

Miss Louise was going to try satisfying Katherin's request while applying her skills as a governess to appease the young lady's fear of not displaying her finest demeanour during the ball.

Katherin felt quite pleased with herself for devising such an elaborate plan to solve her dilemma, and perhaps not disappointing her father. She had hoped that this particular evening would be the perfect one, from which all others would be measured. She spent the rest of the morning studying Miss Louise's next set of instructions with more vigour and dedication.

Once the governess returned with word, she sought to speak with Katherin. Katherin was so delighted to hear that she'd been invited to the elegant Mrs. Rush's soirée where countless debutantes would be attending, that she simply forgot herself and embraced Miss Louise with feverish gratefulness.

Later that week, Miss Louise assisted Katherin with her dress and all the necessary attire to attend such an eventful evening, allowing Katherin to taste the delights and witness the manners that other young women possessed.

Chapter 3

The soirée began with the arrival of many elegant members of society, counting quite a few ladies dressed in exquisitely flowing gowns and gentlemen attired of their finest suits and jackets. The streetlights were candescently lit, providing a soft hue for the walkway to the entrance of the Rush's home. Katherin had not had the opportunity to participate or even witness such an occasion before tonight. This evening would provide her with the desired experience to prepare her for next week's big introduction.

Katherin had donned a beautiful blue-laced gown that flowed in soft pleats down to her heels. She wore her mother's string of pearls that only accented the fine lace along the neckline of her gown. However elegantly she was attired, Katherin felt incredibly nervous, while her heart raced with excitement. As she stepped up to the entrance of the Rush's residence, she smiled a beautiful smile that displayed her utmost pleasure. This evening was the occasion where she would pay close attention to the social graces, etiquette and demeanour that she had only this evening to perfect. Should it not be for her heart racing, Katherin would have been better equipped to fulfil the assignment that she so eagerly undertook.

Miss Louise had told Katherin that Mrs. Ellen Ellisford would be in attendance. She was to extent her gratefulness for Mrs. Ellisford's generosity for providing Katherin with the companionship during the entire evening. Mrs. Ellisford was a distant relative of the Hampton family. She curtsied in front of many of the guests, while keeping a watchful eye for Cousin Ellen. Katherin was certain to have remembered her cousin even though much time had passed since she had last laid eyes on her. Katherin had hoped her cousin would be at the main entrance to greet her, however, after a long search, she could not find her. After greeting other beautiful young debutantes along with their families, she finally spotted Ellen and two other women who were seated around a table set up with an array of sweets and tea. At first, Katherin noticed that Ellen had gained a considerable amount of weight, perhaps after her first child had been born. The Hampton's had not seen their cousin since the passing of their mother, which occurred before the birth of Ellen's first child. Ellen stood up and came to Katherin, arms extended. "Oh my dear, so excellent to see you and so glad you could make it."

Katherin was taken aback. Yet, she returned the light embrace and 'pretend' kisses on both cheeks.

As she sat down, Katherin reflected that she had seen so many refined guests with perfected social allure, that she feared elegance would not easily be attainable for her.

To her relief, Katherin's heart finally stopped racing. As a result, she could now observe how other girls held themselves. She vowed to practice the correct posture for the entire evening to avoid yet more criticism from Miss Louise. *It would certainly bring a smile to Papa's lips.*

"How do you do, my dear Katherin," Mrs. Maryanne Rush exclaimed with flurry as she approached the table where Katherin and Ellen were seated. "How is your father?"

Katherin stood up in one bound. "Oh, he is fine, thank you, Mrs. Rush. He also sends his appreciative regards for extending an invitation to me in such a short notice," she replied.

"I thank you. Tell your father that I am well, and that I send him my best thoughts," Mrs. Rush said with a benign smile crossing her lips. "So glad to see you, Mrs. Ellisford. A delight that you could chaperon Miss Katherin Hampton. Enjoy your evening," she added as she turned to leave the ladies to their happy chatter and to mingle with her other guests.

"I am so pleased that you could join us, Cousin Katherin, and I will be very pleased to be at your disposal for the evening, my dear cousin," Ellen added.

"I am so grateful to you, Cousin," Katherin said, all smiles. She felt confident she could ask many questions regarding what was required of her as a debutante.

The evening proceeded with little incident. At one point, some of the ladies gathered in one corner of the vast ball room for personal reasons. Many young women were displaying their finest gowns with airs that confirmed that Katherin possessed only very few of the refinement necessary to secure her future. Although convinced that she needed to display herself with grace and elegance, Katherin felt strongly that her mother had taught her to appreciate life with a loving heart. This message was far more important to her. It was of greater import to have love for one another, rather than how you held yourself in public. However, Katherin felt it was necessary for her to pursue her study of societal conduct and etiquette, since the next event would require graceful sophistication and perfect demeanour on her part.

Cruel Providence

Ellen introduced her young cousin to her many acquaintances who attended the soirée. All the while Katherin remained on display. She could only wonder if this is what she was born to do – good breeding stock was only intended for show – whereas men came to gaze and ponder whether this was the right one for their personal use, as cattle are on display at an auction for the farmer to examine before he placed a bid, and the highest bidder would take the prize home. Is this what an accomplished woman had to look forward to? Katherin didn't want this to happen to her. She would rather remain in her father's home, taking care of family matters as her mother had done before her. As Katherin thought of her dearly departed mother, a tear forced itself out of the corner of her eye. She then excused herself and rushed to the powder room to dab her eyes before she ruined her perfectly powdered face. While she was walking towards the ladies' salon, Katherin ran into a gentleman who presented his excuses before introducing himself only as William. He was definitely handsome, but it was his charm that Katherin found breathtaking. William had aristocratic features; a strong jaw line with periwinkle blue eyes, dark brown brows, hair the colour of sunlight. The dimples in his cheeks seemed to mock and smile before he did. He was by far the most handsome gentleman in attendance. She curtsied, excusing herself before anyone noticed her tears, which were now running down her cheeks. She wondered if excusing herself so abruptly was the proper thing to do, or perhaps she ought to have no emotions whatsoever? The world, with all its proper or improper behaviours, was more than Katherin was prepared for, or could understand at this time. This only persuaded her that she was totally unprepared to cope during her first public appearance. She knew that she would soon be attending her first formal social event with many she would not know, and the whole affair seemed too ridiculous the more consideration she gave to it.

After restoring her face as best she could, Katherin returned to the ball room, desperate to find her cousin and sit quietly for the remainder of the evening with no other incident. However, as she crossed the room, William intercepted her and requested her name. Katherin not knowing what the conversational rules were, curtsied and gave him her first name before she evaded further conversation and rushed to rejoin Ellen. After returning to her table, she could still feel William's eyes upon her. To Katherin's total dismay, Ellen had observed this transgression that was completely improper. Ellen did not waste any time to warn her young cousin of this impropriety in the exchange with William. Katherin was so distraught at being reprimanded in public that she felt as though she would sink through the marble floor from embarrassment. Not wishing further discomfiture for the duration of the soirée, it would dearly suit her to hide away for the rest of the evening. She also wondered if her Papa would be prejudiced against her once the news reached his ears.

Feeling as though she had done no wrong by simply giving out her name to a stranger, she thought that, had she not replied appropriately to the young man's request, she would have sounded offensive if not disobedient. She had felt obliged to reply out of respect. She could not have known she had committed a faux pas, as indeed Mrs. Ellisford proposed. Presently, Katherin wondered why she had not been instructed of these protocols beforehand. It certainly would have indeed saved her from humiliation. Katherin glanced at William. He had undoubtedly placed her on the wrong side of her cousin's good will. Yet, he continued staring in her general direction. He was tall with broad shoulders. Whereas he was not overly handsome, his features were rugged in appearance; he could not be mistaken for any gentleman with simple features either. Truth be told, Katherin felt attracted to this man who had most assuredly enticed her to misbehave upon her first outing. As such, it probably would be her last, should word of her ill manners reach her father's ears. Katherin would definitely speak with Mrs. Ellisford to ensure her silence, pleading with her that she was unaware of such a rule before today.

Ellen drank her tea while sampling the best of the sweets, which were put forth to the guests. She must employ the best chefs in all of England from what Ellen had admittedly voiced to the other guests. Mrs. Ellisford had been increasingly gaining a great deal to her gentile feminine figure. She had plenty of bosoms exploding over the top of her corset, seemingly overly tight. Katherin was indeed the very opposite of her cousin, where she displayed beauty only in her fine-boned figure. She was slim and elegant with nothing less than a youthful figure at the tender age of sixteen. In some ways, Ellen felt somewhat jealous of her younger cousin. She resembled her some months before the children came along. They added delight to her life at the cost of her beautiful stature, which was now a distant memory for her. Ellen stuffed another sweet into her mouth, enjoying herself whilst she spoke of being thin.

"Cousin Ellen, I do believe that if I had been instructed of the rules of not speaking with the young man in question, I most assuredly would not have made such a faux pas had I known. Could I dare ask that you not mention this event to anyone?" Katherin pleaded.

"My dear cousin, I should not be as audacious as to mention this boldness of character to anyone of importance, so rest assured that I may keep our little secret," Mrs. Ellisford answered in between sips of her tea.

"Thank you, Cousin; I do declare that I must be better instructed in the maintenance of decorum. I will make every effort not to disappoint you again." Katherin sighed in relief once Ellen had promised not to repeat the incident to anyone.

"Not to worry, Cousin Katherin. Discretion shall be the order of the day. Any amount of good will shall be bestowed upon you. For the moment, simply enjoy yourself," Mrs. Ellisford said, smiling conspiratorially.

Katherin, with another breath of relief, threw her cousin a gentle smile. She shall not be disappointing to her Papa, nor shame her family with her impudence. She chose to remain calm, by staying close to her cousin, where no eccentric gentleman could turn her world inside out yet again. The evening proceeded with fewer distractions to Katherin's great relief. Her observation of the perfect gentile ladies was most productive; all the while holding herself up with straight back, shoulders pulled back, head tilted slightly upward. Katherin found the posture most uncomfortable and truly ridiculous. *How could one hold such posture for any length of time?* It all seemed artificial just to prove sophistication to others.

Cruel Providence

Why on earth would anyone put herself through such an ordeal? Katherin could only ponder this ridiculous notion. Without a doubt, it all appeared as though society itself had been reduced to austerity at the hands of Miss Louise.

At the end of the evening, as she exited Mrs. Rush's home, however, the same young man who seemed determine to keep his eyes on Katherin, approached her.

"Miss Katherin, may I be as bold as to ask to have a word with you?" William again made another effort to gain Katherin's favour.

"Sir, I do apologize, conversely it may seem quite inappropriate for one to speak with a gentleman while not being properly introduced," Katherin said, while trying to escape into her carriage.

"Yes, I must apologize, Miss Katherin for my forwardness. Then again I would merely request a meeting, with a chaperon, of course, so as to speak with you. Perhaps we could then be properly introduced to one another, thus easing your mind of any inappropriateness?" He most certainly displayed a beautiful set of white teeth when he smiled.

Katherin felt, to her dismay, alarmingly excited with his seemingly genuine request. "I am not positive whether this meeting can be arranged, and I am afraid that I must be departing at once," Katherin told the handsome William. He had the most adorable dimples that were very becoming. To Katherin's horror, she blushed with excitement.

"Miss Katherin, may I ask for your name so as to call upon you, perhaps in the very near future?"

However, Katherin being already seated in her carriage was thus carried away before she had the chance to reply. She was disappointed for not being so brave as to allow William to call upon her. For now, she feared never to see him again had she not been so fearful of disappointing her Papa, that is should news reach his ears of yet another encounter with the elusive man.

The return trip was quite uneventful, as Katherin yawned, wondering whether she would be welcomed at her residence by her loving family. The hour was late and no doubt her siblings would be fast asleep, leaving her Papa seated by the fireplace smoking his pipe.

Her father was ever so gentle, but of late seemed more prone to tears after the bereavement. Katherin would have loved to speak to her sister, Maggie, with whom she'd been very close. Katherin would have spoken to her in regards to the young, handsome man she encountered this evening. Maggie would have surely understood how Katherin felt towards speaking with him while her heart had assuredly led her astray. She so yearned to be with Maggie for just a moment. At present with only the governess for her to confide in, Katherin felt certain speaking with her would prove disastrous. Miss Louise would indeed speak with her Papa, who would reprimand her and would probably lock her up for the remainder of her days. Her carriage approached her home in the country where the coach came to a full stop. The driver helped Katherin out, and escorted her inside. She thanked him for his helpfulness, closing the front door on him. She stood there wondering what information would be best to share with her father before entering the parlour, where Mr. Hampton was waiting for her. Her nervousness was naturally obvious. She sighed heavily before entering the room.

"Hello, Papa!" Katherin let out with open arms while approaching him.

Mr. Hampton smiled at his little girl, who was dressed like an angel. Had she not spoken, he would have thought she was his wife.

"Oh! My dear little one, how are you this evening? Did you enjoy yourself?" he asked, after realizing it was his daughter who had spoken to him.

Katherin bore a striking resemblance to Mrs. Hampton. Edward Hampton would spend long hours remembering where he had first seen his beautiful bride in the garden of his aunt's residence, who was hosting a get-together to celebrate her anniversary to her husband, Frank. The garden was at its most magnificent moments with Constance seated among the beautiful roses. Such elegance among red roses was not for the weak-hearted, for he took one look at her before falling hopelessly in love.

"Yes, Papa, I did have a delightful evening with Cousin Ellen. She was most charming, and warm hearted. Thank you for allowing me to go out," Katherin said, knowing that he would love to hear more details regarding the evening's activities.

Katherin sat with her father for a few moments, feeling the warmth from the fireplace before kissing him goodnight and retiring to her bedchamber for a restful night.

Once upstairs, Katherin undressed and prepared herself for bed. She turned the covers down and then slipped under them, where she stayed warm while she dreamed of William. She had no idea as to who the young man could be. However, she was unable to rid the embedded memory of the young man's face and penetrating eyes from her mind. Katherin closed her eyes once more, falling fast asleep while dreaming of the gentleman who had captured her heart.

Chapter 4

The following week, on the morning of the ball, Katherin awoke fairly early to prepare for her debut into high society. She had butterflies in her stomach, which prevented her to have breakfast with the family. Nevertheless Katherin smiled, which was a fair indication that she would be feeling fine to attend this evening's ball. She rose from her seat, walked to her Papa, and kissed him on the forehead.

Mr. Hampton simply accounted her loss of appetite to a nervous stomach, which would remedy itself once the soirée was underway. On the other hand, his daughter may have another reason for being anxious after he divulged the surprise he had kept secret from her. Mr. Hampton had hoped she would be quite excited, for what he was about to tell her the following day would change her life indefinitely. He imagined she would be quite astounded with the news, and perhaps not eat for a week from the shock. He smiled to himself as he truly wanted Katherin's happiness at heart, and what better way to do that than to secure her future.

After excusing herself, Katherin exited the dining hall and returned to her bedchamber to begin the slow transformation of a girl to one of a woman now that she had come of age. She had some measurable reservations however. She wondered how one could go from a girl to a woman without the proper time to prepare, as though it could happen with a swish of a wand. *How does society expect such a transition,* she thought? However so, she would do her best to please her father, no matter how senseless it might seem. If her mother had been present, Mrs. Hampton would have guided young Katherin to do what was right all the while helping her to understand what were her innermost feelings regarding her transformation. She could not help but reflect on the two individuals she most dearly missed, and a new appreciation of matters of the heart that emerged with fond memories. And had they both been granted one wish, Katherin was convinced that they would return to earth, as they would not miss her debut. Consequently, because this was not possible, she would take them both in her heart to the soirée. After warming her heart with this notion, she could embrace her new escapade, persuading herself that she would enjoy the evening regardless of her inner fears.

Miss Louise entered the room. "Good morning, Miss Katherin," she said.

"Good morning to you too, Miss Louise. The day has finally come, hasn't it? I am truly grateful for your assistance in transforming the simple and awkward girl I once was into the elegant woman that will surely please Papa."

"My dear Katherin, you should choose to be happy for yourself. This would most certainly please your Papa," Miss Louise pointed out to Katherin. "Do you not agree?"

"I believe you are correct. The transformation will better suit my position, thereby fostering my father's pleasure while fulfilling my obligations. I do believe my feelings are of happiness as well," Katherin replied.

"Yes, I do believe you are. You should not be so fearful of the evening however. You shall do quite well, my dear. You may not have noticed that throughout the past year you have grown into a most lovely young woman, blossoming as you have. I believe you are equipped for this new phase in your life, and I have it on good authority that your Papa is very pleased. I know this because your father has planned a small surprise for you later." Miss Louise seemed to make efforts to calm the fearful young woman. She hoped that the encouragement would enable Katherin to take a leap towards the first stage of womanhood more easily.

"Why, Miss Louise, I do declare! How fantastic is this news you bring me. I am very pleased to hear Papa is happy, and a secret!" Katherin exclaimed gleefully.

Miss Louise, along with a maid prepared the soft white gown to fit a debutante for her first step into society. The neckline of her gown was cut a little lower than usual, showing her bosom and emphasizing her tiny waistline. The gown looked perfect on Katherin's petite frame. Her hair was expertly coiffed while paying close attention to the current style, placing pink pearls amid the many curls combed delicately atop her head, adding a few years to her youthful beauty. Katherin wore her mother's jewels; this time, it was a brilliant diamond necklace that was placed around her delicate neck.

Once the preparations were complete, Miss Louise led Katherin to face the mirror. Katherin saw herself for the first time. She was in awe, for the transformation was absolute. A woman had emerged out of a young girl's awkward body. Katherin could only admire herself in the mirror's reflection. She could not believe how Miss Louise had accomplished such a deed. She was simply speechless at the makeover.

"How have you managed this amazing transformation?" Katherin queried as if she were glancing at someone other than herself. She was in such disbelief at her reflection that she blinked to see whether the glass had mistaken the image. "This cannot be me in the looking glass, Miss Louise?"

"My dear Katherin! Your mother would be so pleased at your maturity that she, too, would be elated and possibly speechless. You are truly gorgeous, my dear!" Miss Louise sounded quite pleased with herself and with the results of her tireless work.

"Truly, Miss Louise, you have outdone yourself, and I am sure Papa will be pleased with what you have achieved," Katherin added, quite delighted indeed.

"Now before we see your father, I would very much like for you to eat something as I fear you will faint at the least movement."

"Yes, you may be right. I will try a little; although I cannot eat much in this corset, since there is little room for much else than a small bite. Breathing is most difficult and dancing will definitely prove to be a little challenging." Katherin had great reservations as to what she might be able to accomplish before the night was over.

The afternoon passed very quickly for the ball would begin in less than one hour's time, leaving little time for the last minute preparations. Katherin slipped into her new shoes and commenced her slow descend down the staircase of their house.

Her father was standing at the bottom of the stairs. Mr. Hampton was staring as she descended.

"Constance, is that you?" he instantly questioned, looking as though he had seen a ghost. He glanced away for a moment then back to Katherin. He was white with fright with this last thought.

"Papa! Are you not feeling well?" Katherin queried, while watching her father turning pale with disbelief. He truly believed he had seen his dearly departed wife rather than his own daughter.

"Katherin, you look so radiant and resembling your mother so, that I mistook you for her! You look absolutely stunning, such as your Mama did not so long ago," he added, making efforts to calm himself, while making amends to his daughter for mistaking her for his own bride.

Then again one could not blame him, for even Miss Louise had noticed the remarkable resemblance.

"Yes, Papa, tis I who you see, and not the vision of Mama. Are you feeling alright?" she again questioned, somewhat alarmed at her father's paleness.

"Yes, Oh my! Katherin you are so lovely. Are you prepared to come away for the evening?"

"Yes, Papa. Miss Louise has truly outdone herself, transforming my simple life into one of a princess, I do believe."

"Yes she has. I will call for the carriage, and prepare quickly to escort my lovely girl to the ball of the season," he announced to Katherin while Miss Louise looked on from the top of the stairs.

"Thank you, Papa. I feel somewhat nervous at the prospect," Katherin added, fearing that she would fall faint from fright at any moment.

"Yes, I certainly understand. Do not fear, but feel the thrill of it all, for this is one of the most exciting evenings, other than that of your marriage, of course," he put in, allowing his words to lift his daughter's spirits.

"Yes, thank you, Papa," Katherin said while her father went to see that the carriage was standing in front of the doors.

They both left for the debutante's ball where Mr. Hampton was somewhat quiet, not expressing his emotions. He found himself in deep thought, for no doubt he wondered how he would go on without his eldest daughter. He had already lost two members of his family in the past year, and now, he was quite aware that he would be losing another child fairly soon.

Chapter 5

The carriage pulled up to the large estate where many
other carriages opened their doors to let out gorgeous
young women and their families. Katherin's first sight
of the property was of the huge, round columns
announcing the imposing grandeur of the structure
which they supported. It seemed as if these giants
were inviting guests to enter the estate with style and
grace. Katherin could not do anything but stare in
amazement at the grandeur of this house. The
walkway lights illuminated the way to the entrance
with hopes of a magnificent evening for Katherin's
coming out ball. She felt as though all who came
within her proximity would hear her heart beat. She
therefore devised a plan to stay relatively clear of
most who may witness her fears. Katherin's father
smiled at her amazement before assisting her down
from the carriage with his arm outstretched. He thus
escorted Katherin inside the house as any proud father
would. He witnessed Katherin glancing everywhere
in total wonder. And for him to put her in the
limelight was outstandingly rewarding. Mr. and Mrs.
Hampton wanted their children to grow up with
simplicity to prevent them from being exposed to a
merciless public life. Constance once had been
scrutinized to such a degree that it had become totally
unnatural. They wished for a much more
uncomplicated lifestyle for their children.

Entering the mansion with all the elegance of a
princess even though she was not brought up as such,
Katherin had that regal look about her as her mother
had once possessed. Mr. Hampton looked so very
honoured this evening. He was an elderly gentleman

who was still spry for his age. His grey eyes were dimmed with sadness, but could still twinkle when he smiled, and this evening he had much for which to be pleased. His dark hair greying at the temples gave him a distinguished air. His handlebar moustache hid his full lips and gentle smile. He smiled, bowing with every introduction. He was not as dashing as his younger brother had been, but he could carry an air of respect. He was attired of the finest embroidered waistcoat, breeches and had his head covered of a beautiful silk wig – he was impeccably groomed.

Katherin and her father were escorted to the top of the grand staircase descending to the main hall where Mr. Hampton gave their names to the major d'homme, who was dressed as though he were himself a prince. He tapped the floor three times with his cane to announce their arrival to the assembled company: "Mr. Hampton and Lady Katherin Hampton D'Amico, daughter of the late Princess Constance D'Amico."

Katherin was startled. After they stepped down the majestic stairs and approached their hosts, Katherin curtsied while her father bowed in front of the duke and duchess. They then walked away toward the grand ball room, Katherin with her hand on her father's arm.

Katherin turned to her Papa. "Why did you not tell me that Mama was a princess? Why would you not do so?" Katherin had a hard time understanding why her father had never told her.

"Dear Katherin, we both felt that a public life, to which your mother had been subjected in her youth, would not be in our children's best interest. Therefore, we both decided not to inform our children. It was a decision we made long before you were born."

"Is this the secret Miss Louise has mentioned earlier this morning?" Katherin queried with delightful curiosity and excitement.

"That is but one. I have one more to offer later, my dear one."

They both entered the grand ballroom, bowing and curtsying to the Duke and Duchess of York, along with the many guests in attendance at the ball of the season. At that moment, Katherin could not help but feel quite self-conscious. She wanted to be as perfect as her mother had been. For the first time, Katherin understood why her mother had such regal posture and demeanour. *How could they have not mentioned such a thing to me before today?*

As she made her way across the floor of the immense ballroom, Katherin wondered whether she was as graceful as her mother had been. Her father turned to Katherin and smiled.

"Now, my dear, I want you to have a wonderful time tonight. You will remember this evening for the remainder of your precious life." He grinned at her. "But it is time for you to open your dance card and meet a few of the young admirers waiting to whisk you away."

"Papa, please do not make fun of me this evening," Katherin said, a little overwhelmed.

"No, I would not make fun of you, my dear. I simply want you to enjoy yourself."

"Yes, of course, Papa."

Mr. Hampton then introduced his daughter to Mr. Chester Manors among many other gentlemen they met that evening. Mr. Manors escorted Katherin onto the dance floor where she took her first steps, dancing with a gentleman. She felt she had danced fairly well since this had been her first, although she did not feel comfortable with Mr. Manors. His hands roamed a little more than they should have. After which Katherin was introduced to a few other gentlemen whom she listed on her dance card after meeting them. They danced a minuet and a few other pieces of entertaining music played by a discreet but first rate orchestra. It was as though she had gone to heaven, and at any moment, Katherin was certain that her mother and sister Margaret would come down the stairs to join them both at the most glamorous time of young Katherin's life. Tonight, she truly felt her mother's presence, her spirit guiding her along each dance move. Could this be a dream, and at any moment, she would wake to find herself back in her bedchamber fast asleep?

An hour later, Katherin begged to sit out the next few dances to rest her tender feet. She could not remember the last time she felt so weary, yet she was enjoying herself. Across the room, Katherin could see her father speaking to Mr. Manors. She wished never meeting him again. She could not help but feel that Mr. Manors was not simply interested in dancing with her either. He seemed to have other intentions for a more pleasurable evening with Katherin. She turned away once Mr. Manors glanced her way for fear he would suspect her willingness to dance with him again. She even crossed his name out of her dance card with some anger. As Katherin turned away, she found herself staring directly into the eyes of a young man. Her heart began to race. She smiled ever so slightly. It was then that she felt someone tapping on her shoulder.

"Miss Katherin! May I be so fortunate to have the next dance?" he asked her.

Katherin remembered being introduced to the man, and desperately wanted to remember his name, but couldn't for the life of her.

"Yes, that would be nice," she heard herself reply without further thought.

"Yes, thank you, Miss Katherin. You do remember my name, do you not? Not to worry, I am certain that you have been introduced to many young men this evening. I am Count Leanard of Sussex."

"Yes, Count Leanard. I do remember Father making the introduction with Miss Mary Leanard also, is that not correct?" Katherin countered.

"Yes, she is my sister if you recall."

Katherin rose from her seat with some reluctance to dance with the count. She gave a slight smile out of courtesy, but glanced back to where the young man had been. He was no longer in sight. While dancing, Katherin attempted to glance around the room in search of the elusive young man that had captivated her attention. She was not so fortunate as to locate him however. It was as though he had vanished from the room.

The dance ended and not a minute too soon according to Katherin's feet. She felt as if her feet were beginning to be more painful while her corset grew tighter around her chest. At this particular time, she would have preferred to be sitting for the rest of the evening. She looked around her for her father so that he could escort her to the powder room, wherever it may be. She dearly wanted to escape a few more dances. She was obviously tired.

"Oh, Papa, there you are. I have been wishing for your assistance." Katherin smiled ever so faintly.

"Yes, my dear, what can I do for you that any of the many young men here could not?" he replied. He had questioned her in a manner that Katherin was now wondering why he was behaving differently all of a sudden.

"Papa, would you be as kind as to escort me to the powder room?"

"Why, my dear, if this is the sole purpose for your query, by all means let us be quick as I do profess there will be countless young men who may perish should you not return in a timely manner."

"Thank you, Papa. However, I will take a few extra moments in the powder room. My shoes are hurting my feet," Katherin told her father while she limped ever so slightly towards the ladies' restrooms to seek relief.

"Would you prefer that I escort you home, my dear?" he asked her out of concern.

"Why no, Papa, I simply require a few moments' rest, that is all." She knew that she had to speak with the young man who had eluded her before she would let her father take her home.

Katherin closed the door, relieved that she was alone for the first time this evening. She sat on the bench, resting her sore feet with her footwear removed. She wondered how they could produce such a pair of slippers without consideration of how they would affect the unfortunate woman who wore such a shoe. Katherin could only ponder the logic behind the making of this apparel. After resting for what seemed a short time, Katherin rose to glance at herself in the looking glass. She felt as though she required Miss Louise's magic fingers to repair the damage to her hair. She decided to fix it to the best of her abilities, which of course took a little more time than she originally expected to spend in the restroom.

Upon returning to the ballroom, she glanced around for her father but he was no longer in sight. She felt someone tapping her on the shoulder. As she turned towards the person, she found herself facing the young man on whom she had pinned great hopes of meeting again. It was William.

"Miss Katherin, I truly thought I would not have the privilege of setting my eyes upon you again. But fate has been kind. I am thrilled to have the privilege to be in your presence tonight. Would you be as kind as to grant me the next dance?" William spoke to Katherin as if they had known each other since childhood.

For Katherin, time stood still. She blushed from his beautiful words that were whispered to her so gently. "Why yes, of course, William. By all means, let's have that dance," Katherin replied excitedly, forgetting her manner of speech completely. They danced to the music of a *Contredance* for a few moments, but unfortunately it was nearly over.

"Could I please have the next dance, Miss Katherin?"

"Why, Mr. William, I would be delighted to dance with you yet again."

They both danced around the entire ballroom floor as though they were floating on air. Once again time stood still, when Katherin's dreams seemed to materialize from outer space. However, their moment in time came to an end with the last note. William asked for one more dance.

"I would have loved to dance with you again, should my slippers not be so very tight, that is. Thus,

I must beg out, Mr. William. I am terribly sorry," Katherin pleaded gently.

"Why yes. However I do feel terrible that someone so beautiful may be in such pain. I am also saddened with the thought of not dancing with you earlier this evening. I would carry you away should your father not duel for your honour, my fair lady."

"Mr. William! I do believe you are teasing me. I must now return to my father's side, however pleasant it may have been to remain here with you," Katherin said, her heart filled with delight.

Yet he stopped her before she ran off. "I apologize, Miss Katherin, if I sound inappropriately forward, but I do believe we have not been properly introduced. Once we are, I most certainly will request another dance."

At this precise moment, Katherin's father appeared to rescue her apparently from yet another dance partner.

"Katherin, my dear! Come with me, I believe it is time to share my secret," Mr. Hampton said, obviously trying to save Katherin from more injury from another suitor, who she had not had the privileged to meet yet. He prided himself on knowing everyone at the ball, but the name of this young man, standing in front of his daughter, had even eluded his memory.

"I apologize, Father, but I would love to hear what you have kept from me. I cannot believe you could have retained such a secret," Katherin smiled with fondness to her loving father.

"Come with me and I will introduce you to someone of great importance."

Mr. Hampton escorted his daughter across the floor before reaching a circle of ladies and gentlemen who were standing chatting amongst one another. "Excuse me ladies and gentlemen. I would love for you to meet Lady Katherin Hampton, my eldest daughter. Katherin this is Mr. and Mrs. Hendrix, Mr. and Mrs. Shore and over here is Count Leanard to whom you have been recently introduced." Her father nodded to each one of them as he spoke their names. Out of respect, they bowed to one another.

"It is a pleasure to meet you," Katherin said while curtsying.

"Now, my dear Katherin, I would love for you to dance with Count Leanard for he has anxiously waited to have another dance with you." Mr. Hampton took Katherin's hand and placed it on Count Leanard's arm.

"It is a pleasure to have another dance with you, Miss Katherin."

"Likewise, Count Leanard," was the only reply Katherin could muster after what had in effect transpired. Katherin was somewhat confused with the introductions, especially since her father had not informed her of his little secret. However confused she felt, she was led out towards the dance floor where she danced in the company of someone toward whom she felt reticent. As the music began, the count and Katherin had a moment to look in one another's eyes. Katherin felt she had seen recognition in his gaze, but this only managed to alarm her. Once the music ended, they soon returned to the circle of friends.

"Now, Papa, I was certain you had some news for I have been patiently waiting." She was beyond patience to hear this secret.

"Yes, my dear Katherin, I do indeed have excellent news for you."

"Yes, Papa?"

"Count Leanard of Sussex has made an offer of marriage. You will be happy to know that your father has generously accepted this nobleman's offer."

"Papa, I do not know what to say. May we have a word in private, please, Papa?" Katherin was truly taken aback at this revelation, and only wanted answers while feeling that her whole life was caving in under her sore, tired feet.

"Why yes, my dear. You must have many questions for me." They both bowed out of the group. Mr. Hampton escorted Katherin to the balcony outside, where Katherin could, at last, take a breath of fresh air before she collapsed in front of the entire gathering of guests.

As they reached the balcony, Katherin spoke firmly. "Papa, how could you? How could you accept a marriage proposal on my behalf?'

"Katherin, you will see that this marriage will be very beneficial to you and your family. The count is a very prominent figure in social circles. I have it on good authority that he is very wealthy, and can be very kind."

"Papa, I can not marry him. I am not on familiar terms with the count. I cannot marry someone I know not. How could you even contemplate accepting a proposal of marriage on my behalf without so much as informing me of your decision beforehand, Papa?"

"I beg of you to calm yourself, my dear. Do you suppose that your Papa would not carefully consider the best for his lovely daughter? So I insist that you refrain from arguing my decision at once. We will continue this conversation in days to come. Now, do not fret and let me see your lovely face. There, there, I will wipe the tears away. And now we ought to return to the dance floor afresh before we must take our leave for the night. Let Papa see your beautiful smile one more time. There that is most becoming of a lady," Mr. Hampton went on, encouraging Katherin to relax while returning to the guests with a tentative smile draped over her lips.

"Yes, Father," Katherin replied with no tone of amusement in her voice. She was yet again led to the ballroom to seek out the next partner listed on her dance card.

"Now my dear, won't you dance with Count Leanard before we take our leave."

"Yes, Papa," Katherin replied with obvious resignation.

Count Leanard escorted Katherin for one last dance. They momentarily glanced at one another before standing face to face for another minuet. Katherin was amiable, although forced a smile with a great deal of effort as she danced with her partner. They were crossing the dance floor and changing partners when her eyes happened to land on William. Their gazes were filled with sparkles of love. Katherin felt a stir in her that she hadn't felt before. His gaze was ever so subtle lasting no more than a moment, but Katherin knew she must do whatever it took to be properly introduced to him before she was whisked away perhaps to marry a man she did not even know. Fear gripped her as she finished the dance with the count. They bowed at one another, and then he kissed her hand, producing a very unsettled feeling within her. The count brought her back to her father and he spoke ever so softly in her father's ear. She could only imagine what was being said. She paused for the count to leave before asking her Papa to come with her.

"Papa, I beg you to introduce me to a particular gentleman so that I can at the very least know his full name."

"Why my dear, you are not in need of another suitor. However, if it would please my little one, I will oblige." Mr. Hampton walked with Katherin up to William, the two men eyeing each other curiously. They bowed at one another before Mr. Hampton said, "I would like to introduce my eldest daughter, Miss Katherin Hampton to you, sir. And you are?" Mr. Hampton paused, allowing for the introduction to proceed.

"I, my good sir, am Mr. William Hampshire." He glanced at Katherin with a sparkle in his eyes. He bowed in front of Katherin. "It is a pleasure to greet you, sir, and your lovely daughter."

"I would say this is a pleasurable moment for both of us, too. However, Miss Katherin is soon to be engaged, and therefore I cannot allow you to call on her in the future," Mr. Hampton added with a smirk on his face that clearly upset Katherin.

"Papa, I was under the impression that we were to have a discussion in regards to…?" Katherin said, desperately avoiding giving the wrong impression to Mr. Hampshire.

"I must confess to you that my daughter does not understand the protocol of society, which has been handed down over generations. As you can see we have indulged in her upbringing. Now, Katherin and I will beg your forgiveness as we are to take our leave from this wonderful night."

Mr. Hampton bowed turning to exit the room. Katherin was forced to leave with her father, while he took her arm. Katherin felt her life falling apart. She glanced one last time over her shoulder to see if young William Hampshire was looking in her direction. He was. She gave him a smile before they quickly vanished through the main doors towards their carriage.

The carriage ride home was spent largely in silence. Katherin could still see Mr. Hampshire's eyes locked on hers. She was determined to persuade her father that she should not marry the count. She felt not the slightest inclination toward Leanard de Sussex, and could not conceive a life with him, title or no title. She was determined that he would not make her happy, and was quite convinced she could never bring happiness to him either. They would only live in sheer agony should her father insist on their marriage. Katherin wished dearly for her mother to be present, as she was confident that she would not agree to such an arrangement.

Mr. Hampton was also in deep thought while the carriage continued its course to their estate. He was most ardently concerned about his daughter, and could not conceive why she would not want to marry the count. Any woman would be thrilled to have such a proposal of marriage from a man who could provide every amount of security imaginable. *How could she behave in such a manner?* Perhaps, he was guilty for her attitude. He likely had pampered his children in excess after his wife's passing. He must stay strong for his eldest daughter would certainly make an enormous mistake should she not marry Leanard de Sussex. *On the other hand, when marrying the count, she will be very happy with such a marriage agreement, and therefore pave the direction for all our other children's future.*

They pulled up the front entrance. Mr. Hampton stepped down from the carriage while assisting his daughter down. They both entered the front door in a sombre mood. Katherin yawned, and then mentioned how exhausted she felt. She immediately removed her shoes before going up the long staircase to her bedchamber. As she drew up her gown to climb the stairs, she yawned once more before she reached the top landing. After entering her room, she immediately slipped out of her gown and soon slid under the covers for she desired to dream of William Hampshire for making her the happiest she felt in a long time, regardless if it were only for a few moments. Her only desire now was to persuade her father to change his mind regarding the count. Tomorrow she would certainly put forth an excellent argument that would persuade her Papa that she could decide for herself what was best for her.

Chapter 6

The sun seemed to have risen too early the following morning. Birds were singing outside on the tree branch that overhung near Katherin's window. She was not too pleased to be awakening from her dream of William. While she slept, Katherin did not get any emerging grand plans to stop her father from marrying her off to a man for whom she had absolutely no feeling. The count was so much older than she was, while Katherin being half his age, could not make for a less suitable couple. *How could Papa believe that she would be happy or even content with such an arrangement?*

Miss Louise entered Katherin's bedchamber carrying her gown. She had already drawn a bath for her and she would help her pupil to dress for yet another demanding day. Stepping out of her bed was painful, whereas the appearance of her feet covered with blisters were clear signs of what she had endured the previous evening. However sore she felt, Katherin would not have missed this day for any amount of gold. She only needed to think of Mr. Hampshire to produce a smile on her lovely face.

"Miss Louise, how are you this morning?" Katherin asked, regardless of how she felt.

"Very well thank you," she replied. "Your Papa is expecting you at your earliest convenience. I do pray that we should make haste of your morning routine," she added.

"Why would father be summoning my presence at such an early hour? Is my father impatient for my company?"

"I believe he would like to leave early this day. However, he did not indicate what his intentions were, or his purpose, my dear Miss Katherin."

"I will certainly do my best to accommodate father's request," Katherin replied, while not wanting to upset him, for she desperately had to dissuade him from going any further with his ludicrous idea of marriage between her and the count. Katherin simply wished to remain with her loving family and carry on as usual.

A short while later Katherin entered the study where her father was seated in his favourite chair amongst the countless bookshelves, which illustrated the degree of study her father had done in order to perform his daily duties. He was a very proud man who worked hard to ensure his standing in society, which had become somewhat fragile of late, and which, he knew, could crumble at a moment's notice. One day you could have it all, whereas one small set back, such as losing a spouse could ruin an empire. Mr. Hampton could only relate too well to the fragility the financial world had grown of late as he had experienced first-hand. At the moment, he was aware of what had to be done in order to regain his economic status. Katherin walked to her father's desk on the far side of the room and stood erect in front of his desk.

"Ah, Katherin, my dear! It is very pleasant to see you this morning. I am grateful that you made haste and appeared promptly this morning. Did you have a good evening? I would like to have our breakfast meal together so we can discuss the affair we touched onto last evening," he said before Katherin could answer his first query.

"Yes, Papa, I most certainly had a very amusing time."

Her father rose from the chair. "Let's go to the dining room and talk before your Papa has to leave for a few days. There are urgent business matters that cannot wait, and I must leave at once," he told her.

Katherin could only wonder why her father had to leave so quickly. She also felt uneasy regarding her plan, which would persuade him differently in respect to marrying Count Leanard. "Yes, Papa," she calmly replied.

As they entered the dining room, Mr. Hampton indicated a chair on the right of his own. "Now sit, my dear." As soon as they were seated, the servant brought in the various breakfast items to the table and left discreetly.

"There now," Mr. Hampton said, after helping himself of fried eggs and bread. "I do believe you have been offered a very comfortable life with Count Leanard..."

"Yes, however...," Katherin interrupted, after nibbling on a piece of bread buttered with some fruit preserves.

"No, please, hear me out before you reply, my dear." Her father raised his voice slightly.

Katherin stared at her father, not wishing to cause him any distress at this juncture. She knew that she would stand a fairly good chance at changing his mind if she did not upset him beforehand.

"As I have stated, the count is a very wealthy man, who has earned respect as well as having a kind disposition. You could do no better. So what would be your objection to such a fine match?" he questioned, somewhat assured that there would be none.

"Yes, Father. I believe that should I have only the financial concerns, the count would be a first rate choice. However, that is not the sole reason for marriage as you well know, Papa."

"I am aware that it does require love for one another. However, you do not know the count. Therefore, I have arranged for several meetings between the two of you. As you can appreciate I have thought of the point you made last night regarding the fact that you could not marry a man you did not know. Thus, for the moment, I would like for you to give this your immediate attention and consideration. Would you do this for me, my dear?" he asked her, knowing full well Katherin would have to agree.

"Yes, Papa. I would like to please you, although I would also like to speak with you regarding the young man we met last evening."

"You cannot be serious! I have no knowledge of this young man and therefore would not promote such a union. You have a very respectable offer with a prominent, wealthy man, who, I might add, has made a generous offer. I have arranged an advantageous marriage for you, and thus, we should give a respectable response to his proposal. Do you not agree?"

"Yes!" Katherin sighed, totally defeated in her initial purpose. She fell silent.

"You are to meet with Count Leanard this very afternoon. You must respect my wishes, giving him your utmost esteem. While I do not expect you to give him an answer today, I do expect a highly thoughtful response to his offer in due course. Could you do this for your Papa, and simply consider the offer seriously?"

Cruel Providence

"Yes, Papa. I will consider his offer; however, I do have many reservations regarding this union." Katherin would hold out from giving a favourable answer to his request. She felt strongly about someone else who had her heart beat at a rate unknown to her. She had never experienced such an attraction previously. This strange feeling gave her more incentive to pursue her dreams. Katherin could not help but feel that her father had made many arrangements, which were predetermined. *How could he make all manners of planning without consulting me?* Then again she was aware that this was the social norm. *Is this what growing up means?*

They both left the study, having very little time to enjoy their breakfast. Meanwhile Edward came in with Genevieve and Jane. They sat to have breakfast with Miss Louise. Mr. Hampton told them that he had to leave on urgent business but did not elaborate on the nature of the business. As far as Katherin was concerned, he could be seeking another suitor for her in the event that she remained at odds with him.

After breakfast, the children were sent upstairs where their tutor was expecting them for their day's schooling. They were likely to be studying mathematics or reading. Before leaving the dining room, Genevieve caused a commotion for she wanted to remain at Katherin's side for the rest of the day. Katherin had been exempt from the daily education in favour of preparing herself for yet another meeting with the count. A venture that Katherin was convinced was a waste of time. She sincerely did not want to contemplate doing anything with a man that could easily be her father if age were the principal consideration in this matter.

Katherin would prefer to stay home with her brother and sisters.

The Count of Sussex was shorter than her father with a full head of salt and pepper hair tied at the nape of his neck with a black silk ribbon, and a face adorned of a Greek nose that was larger than she had been accustomed to see. He sported a small, robust belly, but seemed to have developed an ample torso, perhaps from practising sports during his youth. It wouldn't be unreasonable to think that her father may have overlooked the differences in their ages and other serious disparities. *Should he have forgotten this colossal detail? Perhaps he has failed to observe other defects in this relationship.* Katherin could only ponder these thoughts. She decided to investigate other points for it would in all likelihood strengthen her case against the count.

The count's carriage pulled up to the main entrance. The moment came for Katherin to take her leave with the count. Count Leanard came along with a chaperone. Katherin's governess met the count in the foyer and she was introduced to him. They had a few words, exchanging pleasantries, before Katherin was escorted out to the carriage for their trip to the gardens at the town square.

They arrived in town where spring displayed many coloured flowers which only served to enhance the beauty of the scenery. Once they stopped the coach at the town square, the Count of Sussex assisted Katherin down the couple of steps from the carriage. They then began their stroll across the cobbled stones and down the sandy gravel trail of the small park. Following several minutes of silence, the count broke the obvious tension between them.

"Are you comfortable, that is, are you warm enough?" the count asked, displaying some nervousness in his manners.

"Yes, thank you," Katherin answered, not wanting to remain silent while they both seemed to suffer through agonizing moments of tenseness.

"I spoke to your father regarding this arrangement. He seemed quite pleased with the offer. Might I ask what your feelings are toward it?"

Katherin could not help but feel that she was a prize animal at the town's fare where two men had made arrangements to purchase her.

"Initially, I must confess I was shocked to hear of your intent. At the moment, I must say that I am not sure how I feel regarding this *arrangement*." Katherin only wished not to offend him as she emphasized the word 'arrangement'.

"I quite understand, my dear. I do have good intentions toward you and our union. Speaking sincerely, I would prefer receiving your approbation rather than inducing you into a forced marriage. I wish for you all the sweetness that would be brought to a loving match. I am quite fond of you as you may have gathered," Count Leanard confessed.

However, Katherin was not entirely certain of his truthfulness, especially after his statement in regards to having to induce her into a 'forced marriage,' which rang volumes in her ears. This bothered her more than she wanted to admit. She felt certain that her father would not agree to such a union would he hear of the count's intentions to "force a marriage" upon her.

They walked until Katherin felt she could no longer walk on her sore feet, as her footwear had, once again, become most uncomfortable. Yesterday's blisters had not healed yet. The count was companionable and attentive to her every move or expressed desire. Yet, Katherin remained fixated on their age difference and the fact that she did not feel at ease with the man – old or not, she did not like him! She could not for one moment conceive being married to him; even though her father thought the count was a very respectable and gentle man.

They both returned to Katherin's residence with the count escorting Katherin inside the foyer. He then spoke briefly regarding the trip to the museum for the following day. Katherin curtsied to the count before he came up close to her for what appeared to be his desire to kiss her on the cheek. She reacted by stepping back. The count missed her face and had no choice but to kiss the back of her extended right hand instead. He seemed to be offended by her quick reaction. Katherin had never been kissed before, except of course by her family. She could not feel comfortable with the count's quick advances. Therefore, she felt uneasy with the entire encounter.

The count turned to leave, not looking very pleased; however, he did turn briefly, giving Katherin a slight smile. Not wanting to offend the count once more, Katherin reluctantly returned his smile. She did not feel at ease with any of this. In fact she could only shiver as soon as the door was closed upon him. Katherin felt relieved when she was sure he was gone. How would she get through the many engagements that were prearranged, she did not know. If only her father would be here to witness these exchanges for what they truly were. Perhaps then he would accede to Katherin's wishes.

Mr. Hampton was to stay away for several more days. Katherin was unhappy with his absence. She could only wonder what could be keeping him away for such a long time. She knew her father quite well, and he detested being away from home, especially since his wife died. The children also behaved poorly in their father's absence. In the evening when their father wasn't there to read to them, they felt his absence most of all. They so enjoyed their bedtime stories with their Papa. It was the most pleasurable part of their evening. He would always hug the children once the story ended, which gesture offered them the love they so dearly missed since their mother died. Genevieve and Jane would prepare their nightly routine, which was followed with them getting under the covers to wait for their father. They both grew very close to him. The children required more attention from him after their mother and sister's passing. Having their father read to them regularly provided some security in their fragile world.

After a week spent meeting with the count, and reading to the children, Katherin felt exhausted to the point of falling asleep as soon as her head touched the pillow. Of course, the long hours Katherin spent with Miss Louise, learning the various new dances such as the Allemande and Folies D'Espagne were also exhaustive. Katherin could not fathom why it was important for her to know any of these complicated steps.

The week passed with no word from her father. He had been away for a full fortnight. This was so unlike him. Katherin decided to seek out Miss Louise to question her regarding information she may have. Katherin cornered the governess in the study, "Miss Louise, have you not heard word from Papa?"

"Why yes, Miss Katherin. He has sent word just this morning as a matter of fact. He may be detained for a few more days before returning," Miss Louise answered.

"That is so unlike Papa to be away for such a long time," she remarked.

"That is true," Miss Louise agreed.

Katherin left the study to prepare once again to meet with the count. *Could this not end*, she wondered. While preparing herself, Genevieve entered her bedchamber.

"Katherin, how is it that you are not spending time with us while we miss Papa so?" Genevieve asked.

"Genevieve. I have recently spoken with Miss Louise, who mentioned that Papa will be away for a few more nights, which means that he will be with us very soon," Katherin happily told her.

"Why should father be away for so long?"

"I quite agree, he has been away too long. I am certain he misses all of us, and will return at his earliest opportunity." Katherin gave Genevieve a small kiss on the cheek. The little girl smiled before running out of the room. Genevieve was four years younger than Katherin and this was displayed in her manners.

Katherin could only wish to be so carefree. At present, she felt as though her security and all that she held dear to her was crumbling as if made of a house of straw. "Why can we not return to being what was so?" she said to herself.

Soon the count came knocking yet again. He had not missed a single day of courtship with Katherin.

"Ah, Miss Katherin, you look lovely!" he said once they were seated in the carriage and had left the estate.

"Thank you," she replied. "You look quite handsome yourself, Count." Katherin felt obliged to return the compliment although she did without a heartfelt sentiment – only duty.

They both arrived at the count's mansion to meet with his parents. Katherin was rather nervous at the prospect of meeting his family.

She was first introduced to his mother, who appeared to be in her late fifties. Then the count introduced his father. Katherin curtsied to both of them, after which all were directed to the dining room. The count's mother was quite friendly toward Katherin, which was a blessing. His father however appeared to be much more reserved. He gazed at Katherin steadily, which unnerved her. It appeared that the son possessed the same traits of character as the father did.

Countess Stephanie continued to chat with Katherin on their way to the dining room, giving her a chance to feel more comfortable and put Katherin more at ease for the first time since being introduced to the count. The dinner party continued without further incidents. Katherin was questioned regarding her family. It all ended quite amicably. Katherin returned home, but once inside, the count once again made every effort to kiss her. Katherin felt a strong urge to run; in spite of this she forced herself to stand firm, such as an immovable doll would. She blushed as soon as his lips touched her cheek. She wanted to raise her handkerchief to her face and wipe his disgusting saliva off her cheek. She was only too happy to see the count exit her home. Once the door was closed, she sighed with relief before going up to her room.

As she reached the top landing, Miss Louise came out of the children's study and stood unobtrusively behind Katherin.

Katherin swung on her heels, scared out of her wits.

"Miss Louise! You frightened me. Truly! I knew not that you were standing behind as such. Were you spying on our interlude?" Katherin sounded very upset, as if she had just received shocking news.

"I say, Miss Katherin, I surely have not. I was returning to my chambers. It is quite late since I too have been reading stories to the children," she replied, sounding offended.

"I am very sorry, Miss Louise! I have been quite on edge these past few days, and such as you, feeling exhausted in Papa's absence," Katherin said, while making efforts to soften the accusation she threw at her governess.

"Yes, I do believe we have been a little tense since your father's departure. I wish you good night," she said, before turning on her heels and entering her bedchamber.

Katherin turned to her room, entered, and went to sit down by the window before undressing.

While making every concerted effort to forget the past few weeks, she fell asleep with her last thoughts being completely dedicated to William. This gave Katherin a reason to smile once again while dances of adventure roamed freely through her mind.

Chapter 7

Katherin had been dreaming of Mr. William Hampshire and while the remnants of her dream remained in her memory, she smiled with lips delicate as pink coloured roses. In a state of semi-consciousness lazing in bed with the residue of dreams still floating about her mind, William's image soon faded to a distant land, when she overheard such clatter from the Hampton's children where they became much too rowdy for her to remain in bed. She heard laughter and footsteps, along with running, and prancing about the upstairs landing.

"What is happening out there?" she wondered aloud as the children's voices became quite deafening. Katherin could no longer ignore their boisterousness. They should have been at breakfast before they had today's lessons. Was Miss Louise ill perhaps, and where was Mr. Brody, their tutor? Katherin could only speculate. She felt time was wasted lying in bed and decided to rise, dress in her bedside robe, before opening the door to the landing.

Agape, she saw Edward and Jane running about, playing 'catch' along the landing – no governess or tutor in sight.

"Edward, Jane!" Katherin shouted to them. "Please stop this incessant running about. Could you please tell me why you have not gone for breakfast?"

"We have already breakfasted. Why have you not joined us?" Jane replied, still running.

"Merciful! Could you then tell me why you have not joined Miss Louise or your tutor for your lessons?"

"Miss Louise has gone on an urgent matter was all she mentioned, and Mr. Brody has not come in," Jane informed Katherin.

"Don't you recall, sister dear," Edward said, "Mr. Brody is gone for a day's rest?"

"Yes, yes, of course," Katherin replied. "Good gracious," she complained, "where has my mind gone? I will be out in a moment, children. Please return to your study." Then noticing Genevieve's absence, she asked, "And where is your sister Genevieve?"

"She was still eating when we came upstairs, Katherin," Jane replied, poking her brother in the ribs while unable to refrain from laughing with him.

"Yes, of course, I will be out momentarily," Katherin told them. "In the meantime, Jane, be an angel and fetch your sister, will you?"

"Yes, Katherin," Jane said, already running down the stairs with Edward in tow.

Katherin raised her gaze to the ceiling before returning to her bedchamber to wash and finish dressing.

Once ready, she went to the children's study room and resumed teaching their lesson for the day. She enjoyed schooling them. They spent the early part of the morning enjoying each other's company. To Katherin time was very precious, especially in light of the extreme changes that had taken place in her life of late. It was then that Miss Louise entered the room.

"Well, I see you have taken the opportunity to be productive," she told Katherin, while the children giggled amongst them. "I am very pleased to see how Miss Katherin has embarked on a new career," she teased.

"Miss Louise, were you ill and seeking the assistance of a physician perhaps?" Katherin asked.

"No, quite to the contrary. I was called out on an urgent matter that is all. And now that I have returned I will continue teaching today's lessons."

"Yes," Katherin said, although feeling a little perplexed with Miss Louise's explanation.

"Thank you for being helpful, Miss Katherin, but now I think it's time for you to attend to your own chores for the day." Katherin stared for a fraction of a second. "You have instructions in your room to follow for the day," Miss Louise added to a befuddled Katherin before she took her leave.

"Yes, yes, of course," Katherin said with some hesitation.

"Off you go then."

Katherin left the study room reluctantly for what she worried would be another lengthy day with none other than the count. She returned to her bedchamber to fetch her instructions. Picking up the note Katherin read on. To her satisfaction, the note did not mention a word regarding the count, nor any outings with him either. Katherin exhaled in relief. The single instruction was for her to meet with the dressmaker. She gathered her overcoat, and promptly left for the dressmaker's shop with the coach driver.

The driver expertly guided the horses toward town, and once there he parked in front of the shop. He helped Katherin down before escorting her inside. He then climbed back onto the carriage to drive round the corner and patiently waited for his mistress.

Katherin entered the dressmaker's shop and was met by Mrs. Patterson, who was very pleased to see her. Mrs. Margaret Patterson was a plump woman in her early forties with a happy disposition and who laughed at almost everything she said. "Well, Miss Katherin, what would you fancy?" she said while chuckling.

"I am not certain, Mrs. Patterson, perhaps a morning dress with some magenta and white or perhaps the red colour would suit me better, wouldn't you say?" Katherin answered, passing her fingers over some of the dress fabric displayed on the counter.

"That is a fine choice." Mrs. Patterson laughed out loud once more while she retrieved the roll of red fabric. "Let me see how much you've grown, Miss Katherin. Let's take your measurements, shall we? I need to see whether you have grown in more ways than one could possibly hope for." Mrs. Patterson giggled some more.

"I dare say, Mrs. Patterson, I do not eat more than before, at least not in the past few days. I simply have *sprouted* all around.

Mrs. Patterson laughed at Katherin's explanation as if anyone could explain away a young woman's development into adulthood. They chatted for a while as the dressmaker offered pattern ideas from which to choose for not one, but several dresses. It was getting rather late in the morning. Katherin had to leave the shop. When she stepped out of the dressmaker's shop, she accidentally bumped into none other than Mr. William Hampshire.

"Oh! I am so sorry, sir! Oh, Mr. Hampshire! Do forgive me?"

"No, not at all. As a matter of fact, I am delighted to have run into you, Miss Katherin."

"Yes, I am pleased, too, Mr. Hampshire. It is such a serendipitous encounter." Katherin blushed intensely for she felt truly happy for the first time since meeting the elusive Mr. Hampshire.

"Please, do call me William. Could I interest you in a short stroll, Miss Katherin?" he suggested.

"I am not sure, William," she replied. Katherin loved the sound of his name.

"I would be honoured to escort you any place you would wish to go."

"However pleased I may be with your invitation, I must return home for my driver is sitting in wait as we speak," Katherin said, looking up at the coach waiting for her a few paces away from them.

"Then shall I escort you home, Miss Katherin. That is if you please?" he went on.

"Then how would you return to town, Mr. Hampshire?" Katherin asked, showing her uneasiness.

"Now, my dear Miss Katherin, do not worry about me. Besides I have my own means of transport – they will follow me!" he went on, showing his beautiful smile on his handsome face.

"Forgive me; I was simply concerned with your return outing that is all."

"Yes. Then, if you please, I will escort you safely home, Miss Katherin," he stated, rather confident of his victory.

Katherin's carriage rounded the corner to the front of the building to where Katherin and William were waiting for it. Mr. Hampshire assisted Katherin into the carriage and entered with her. They both departed for the Hampton residence seated across from one another. Their journey was one of happiness and quietude that need not be explained. It felt as if little talk was necessary between them. Words could only be whispered. They smiled. Katherin was so excited to have William sitting opposite her that she felt light-headed. She blushed profusely while they, at last, began to converse with one another.

He asked, somewhat nervously, "Miss Katherin, it has come to my attention that you have recently been engaged. Is this information correct?"

Katherin being surprised by his question felt a quick response was necessary. "I do not believe you have been well informed, Mr. Hampshire. An official engagement has not occurred, at least not yet. However, father has suggested he would like a union between the Count of Sussex and me. I have not been able to speak with my father in regards to my personal feelings toward this union.

"I see, Miss Katherin. I thought as much. It is true then that you have been betrothed to Count Leanard of Sussex?"

"Not so, should I have my opinion taken into account. Upon my father's return home, I must persuade him that the union would certainly be disastrous," Katherin blurted, rather ill tempered by this time.

"Do not upset yourself for I too have a plan that may come to your assistance in this delicate situation. I have to confess, Miss Katherin, that from the moment I laid eyes on you, I felt an uncontrollable desire to be with you - I find you irresistibly beautiful – and I find myself thinking about you constantly. I have not been able to think of anything other than to ask you to marry me." All the while William had knelt onto one knee in the carriage while the coach drove toward Katherin's residence.

Katherin was shocked. Without a doubt she hadn't properly processed what had just transpired, but was extremely pleased with William's sudden and truly welcomed proposal. Excluding the disbelief she currently felt, Katherin was momentarily speechless. *Has he presently proposed?* With tongue-tied and unable to form words to answer, she simply stared at William. Katherin could not react with any sense that would indicate her preference either way.

"Miss Katherin, will you not speak to me? I am sorry to have proposed without first providing time for us to get to know one another. However, under the urgent circumstances, I feel that time is precious. I find we cannot delay further. I am not willing to lose you to the Count of Sussex."

"Mr. Hampshire! William, I am not certain as to what to say, for I would love to be wed to you, nonetheless father has yet to be persuaded that such a union is appropriate."

"We have arrived at your residence, Miss Katherin," William said, regaining his seat across from Katherin, "therefore, the time has come for me to take my leave. I do not wish to come away from you for fear of losing you. But for the sole reason that I must leave, since arriving at your home, but should you say yes to my proposal, I will do whatever it takes to persuade your father that I am the better man for you. Do you not agree?"

"Yes, I do." Katherin smiled from ear to ear, feeling the fullness of heart. Could this plan actually work for she had not succeeded thus far in persuading her father of her wishes? Katherin also felt strongly that the count was not fit to be her husband on any account, whereas William Hampshire was genuinely a much superior suitor, not only for his age approaching her, but also for his mild temperament. Katherin could not feel she could be truly happy with the count. So many feelings were rushing through her all at once that she could not utter a single word. Feeling sad to have to depart and merely wishing for the carriage ride to go on forever, this in itself spoke volumes to her.

Then William took Katherin's chin with one finger, lifting her face upward to place a single most gentle kiss on her forehead. Katherin felt a stirring inside her, as if touched by a mild burst of lightning that ran up and down her entire spine. She could see that William felt it as well.

"Then, Miss Katherin, we will gather our strengths to win your father's approval, allowing us to wed. Now we must part from one another, except I will return as soon as I am able to do so, and do not worry, for we shall prevail," William declared, opening his heart to the woman he simply met less than a month ago, but felt he could not live without.

"Yes, I am with you. I will do whatever it takes to persuade my father of our mutual interest and affection. He shall then see that we love one another," Katherin confessed to the young William Hampshire.

The word love had escaped her mouth before she could think, but after it was spoken, she felt relieved. Katherin felt sad to come away; however, upon William witnessing her distress, he leaned close to comfort her. He held her, placing his arms around her shoulders.

"Now please do not be sad. I shall be with you in your heart and you in mine until we join our lives for ever."

William then assisted Katherin out of the carriage, and handed her over to the coach driver, who guided her up the front steps. She turned to have one last look at William before hesitantly closing the door behind her.

"Katherin, where have you been?" Genevieve questioned.

"Ah! You frightened me, and where I've been is a secret," Katherin replied, teasing her younger sister. At that moment, Edward and Jane both came running towards their eldest sister, hugging her as though she'd been away for a fortnight. Katherin could only smile at their tenderness. She also came to the realization that should she wed, she would have to leave her sisters and young brother's company. She particularly found this thought difficult to abide. She would not want to cause any distress to the children. She knew how they missed their mother and sister. Wishing not to create sorrow to her loving siblings, she felt a sense of duty to them by staying with her family, or, at the very least, marry and remain nearby.

Miss Louise soon joined them in the foyer while they still hugged their sister. The little pests were full of chatter. "Now, now children, give your sister room to breathe," Miss Louise said to the little ones.

"It is quite all right," Katherin said, smiling tenderly at her siblings.

"Miss Katherin, how did you do with Mrs. Patterson?" Miss Louise queried.

"May we have a word in private, Miss Louise?" Katherin asked. She wanted to discuss her delicate situation with her governess – the two of them alone.

"Yes, by all means, Miss Katherin. Children, I will join you in the library once I have finished speaking with your sister. Off you go at once!"

The children were at first reluctant to leave, however, they managed to tear themselves away from Katherin's embrace. Miss Louise and Katherin then proceeded into the study where Mr. Hampton usually worked.

"Now what could be such a secret that you wish only to speak of it to me alone, Miss Katherin?" Miss Louise questioned, being relatively curious.

"Yes, I did not want to upset the children by speaking to you in front of them. Mrs. Patterson and I managed to select the fabric required for my new gowns, and she will have the first dress completed the day after tomorrow."

"I have heard word from your father. He will be arriving the day after tomorrow." Miss Louise was happy to inform Katherin.

"That is fine news indeed!" Katherin sounded happy and relieved with the information. "Miss Louise, I do have some distressing affair, which I require to speak with my father. I was wondering whether you could advise me on the matter in question."

"Why yes, Miss Katherin."

"I have been on many outings regularly with Count Leanard and yet I feel strongly that he does not suit me. I have also met someone who would definitely be a far superior suitor. How can I speak with my father in regards to this sensitive situation?" Katherin asked, not wanting to approach her father with less than the ammunition that would best serve her cause.

"Miss Katherin. It is the duty of your father to choose a potential suitor for you. This is the tradition that we, women, have been imposed upon for centuries. Do you suppose you can disrupt such a customary duty because you fancy another? You must have strong reasons for changing your father's good sense."

"I am aware that Papa would choose the suitor, however, I have no desire to marry the count. He is a ridiculous old man. I must confess that I feel ill at ease around this insufferable man!"

"Miss Katherin, you must calm yourself. Upsetting yourself so will not be useful to solving your problem. I understand that you have not had proper time to be acquainted with the count; however, there will be plenty of time for romance after you marry. There is little time before someone weds for such things as romance. I do believe your father has the best intentions for a successful marriage. At best, you may hope for a warm attachment."

"I do not want to marry a man for whom I have no affection and more disgust than anything else in fact. The man even repulses me. How could someone expect me to share the man's bed one day? The proposition is simply preposterous!" Katherin was much distressed with what Miss Louise had suggested.

"Miss Katherin, please do not be saddened or upset, for surely nothing will come from your spent energies. As you well know, your father will speak to you upon his arrival. Perhaps then, you can convey your sentiments to him." Miss Louise made efforts to comfort Katherin. She had become no doubt tense from the entire courtship. "Your father is a very reasonable man, and surely he will listen to you, so do not be distraught."

"Yes, I do pray for compassion and understanding. I believe that Papa has been quite reasonable until the present day. I dearly hope that you are correct in your assumptions."

Chapter 8

At last the day came when Katherin sat patiently waiting for her father's return. Katherin heard some footsteps approaching the front door. She hurriedly made her way to the entrance, where upon the maid opening the massive wooden door, she found not her father but in his place her dressmaker, Mrs. Patterson. While staring at the dressmaker, who was holding the red gown that she had sewn and obviously completed, Katherin looked around her, to see whether her father had also arrived.

"Oh, Mrs. Patterson!" she exclaimed, while still looking around for any sign of her father.

She desperately wanted to speak to him and her patience was running rather thin.

"What is the matter, Miss Katherin?" Mrs. Patterson asked, looking around, too, although not comprehending the reason for Katherin's obvious distress.

"Oh! I was simply looking for my father, Mrs. Patterson."

"Was he to arrive as well at this time?"

"I believe so, that is what I have been told, although I can only wonder what is keeping my father from returning after such a long absence."

"Ah, my dear, I am extremely sorry to provide you with false hopes."

"No, not at all. It was not you, Mrs. Patterson. Please accept my apologies for it is I who should be more sensitive. Here you arrive from town to deliver my gown, in which I cannot wait to be fitted, and I am not receiving you properly. I am not myself today, and I beg for your forgiveness."

"Ah, not to worry, you are very kind, Miss Katherin, as I do understand your disappointment. May I come in to assist you into the gown so that I could make any adjustment necessary before you wear it in public?" Mrs. Patterson offered.

"Oh yes indeed, please do! Do come in, Mrs. Patterson," Katherin said, stepping aside to let the seamstress indoors.

They both climbed to the upper landing, Mrs. Patterson huffing and puffing as she ascended the numerous stairs. She was not as young as she once had been and her body showed signs of aging. Entering Katherin's bedchamber, Mrs. Patterson dropped the gown on the bed, unwrapped it from its linen cloth and assisted Katherin in getting undressed from her morning garments. She then helped Katherin into the red gown with some difficulty – there were yards and yards of fabric to contend with. Katherin was instantly transformed into an elegant woman for she had the most exquisite glow to her face. The red colour reflected its beauty off Katherin's glowing cheeks, producing a fabulous tinge of pink that only silky, flawless skin would reflect.

"Oh my, Miss Katherin, you are a beautiful creature!"

"No, it is not me, but your gorgeous gown. You must have worked the entire night to finish this stunning dress, for it is quite dazzling."

"I thank you for the compliment. You are most welcome and your father will be delighted with how it looks on you."

At that moment, both women heard noises coming from downstairs with children running about. And once again, Katherin hoped it would not be because of a repeat of the disappearance of her governess on another urgent matter. Katherin excused herself to seek the origin of the din.

As she exited the bedchamber, Katherin was astonished to witness what the commotion was all about.

"Oh Papa! I am very pleased to have you return!" Katherin called out. She ran down the stairs as fast as humanly possible, but such a huge gown only hampered her steps.

Mr. Hampton only had a vision of a beauty descending the staircase. He, for not the fact that he was her father, and should he be twenty years younger, would have mistaken Katherin for Constance and marry her all over again. The resemblance was becoming disturbing to him. He shook off the vision and glanced at his daughter.

"Katherin, you are stunning. I am pleased to see you in such a fine gown. You have grown into a refined young lady. It makes me very proud indeed," he declared. However, part of him wished for his wife to return and restore his good nature. It pained him to yearn for her, but more so as he had difficulty appreciating his own child when she reminded him of Constance at every turn.

"Oh, Papa! You are only teasing me!" Katherin uttered as she reached the last step.

Mrs. Patterson rushed down behind her to meet with Mr. Hampton in the foyer.

"Ah, Mrs. Patterson! You have out done yourself. The gown is impressively astounding, and my daughter is a vision to behold!" he complimented the dressmaker.

Mrs. Patterson blushed as if she were a schoolgirl. "It was a pleasure to fit such a handsome girl as Miss Katherin," she stated, laughing nervously.

"Thank you, I do understand what you mean, as I am a proud father indeed!" he went on, and then turned to the other children. "Ah my little ones…. Give your Papa a big hug."

They pounced on their father without further ado. They laughed and truly rejoiced at their father's return. The only one that did not join in was Katherin. She only smiled, visibly delighted with the reunion. Mrs. Patterson chuckled as she prepared to leave.

"Ah, Mrs. Patterson, allow me to escort you to your carriage."

"That would be lovely; then again I do not wish to take you away from the children."

"Not at all, we will celebrate afterwards, and I do need to speak to you regarding another matter," he said on his way out the door.

Katherin was somewhat perplexed with yet another display of secretiveness on the part of her father. The children turned to Katherin finally, having observed her wearing the new red gown adorned with white lace.

"What a beautiful dress, Katherin! Did Mrs. Patterson sew the gown for you?" Genevieve asked.

"Thank you, Genevieve! And yes, Mrs. Patterson fashioned it for me, and this is the reason why I disappeared two days ago," Katherin replied.

Mr. Hampton re-entered the foyer where the children shouted with happiness.

"Did you bring me something, Papa?" little Jane asked.

"Why yes, I do believe I have some gifts for all of you!" he exclaimed.

"Where, Papa, where did you hide them?" Edward and Jane both shouted in unison.

Mr. Hampton pulled at his coat pocket to show the children where he hid the gifts. Jane pulled out a small bag tied with a blue ribbon. Edward did the same, then Genevieve. They untied the ribbons to find candy inside the little purses. As they were placing one in their mouths, Katherin looked on with happiness in her heart. From the time of her debut and with each passing day, Katherin had grown increasingly appreciative of her family. *How dear they are to me, and how much I will miss their joyful laughter*, she thought.

Her father had observed his eldest watching over the children with melancholy.

"My dear Katherin, how are you? You have not come to receive your gift. Why have you not?" he queried, while grinning at her. He had such gentleness about him it was very comfortable. However, the softness of demeanour could not conceal his unending sadness.

"Papa, I am so pleased that we are all together, that is all!" she replied.

"Come and give your Papa a big hug, won't you?"

Katherin crossed the floor and lingered in his kind embrace for a moment.

"Papa, I must confess that I have some rather urgent matters to discuss with you," she whispered in his ear.

"What would you have to tell that cannot wait for me to rest after such a long journey?" he asked her.

"I am so sorry, Papa. How thoughtless of me. You are correct, please accept my apologies," she said, sounding somewhat disappointed with the delay.

"Now, I am sure, we can discuss such things after dinner."

Cruel Providence

Katherin smiled at his offer. "Yes, Papa," she replied, although her father did not miss the obvious disappointment in her voice.

It was a glorious time to have the family reunited. The children were unusually excited, and accordingly, their afternoon lessons with Miss Louise did not prove productive. Katherin went to her room, removed her beautiful red dress, and the lady's maid hung it up. Once the maid left her alone, she took some time to prepare for her conversation with her father later that evening.

There were no particular incidents occurring at dinner, except of course, for the children finally releasing their joyfulness when dessert was served. They were giggling profusely and seemed to have millions of stories to tell their father. Mr. Hampton did not say a word to them regarding their excitability. After dinner, he rose and excused himself to smoke his pipe in peace while relaxing in his study.

Katherin was nervous. She paced the length of the corridor before she dared enter the study. She had a lot to say and explain regarding her decision not to marry the count. She knocked lightly at first, and then louder once she did not receive a response.

"Yes," her father called out.

"It is me, Papa," she said, while pushing the door open.

Mr. Hampton waved Katherin to enter the room.

She walked up to her father and said, "I am glad you are home, Papa. I fear the children and I have missed you so, and of course, they have not been the same since you traveled."

"I must confess that I am delighted to be home, Katherin. I do believe you have some rather pressing matter to discuss with me, nevertheless."

"Yes, Papa, I do. I understand you desire for the count to marry me, and although we have gone on many outings, I have yet to feel any attachment for him. He actually gives me a distasteful feeling that I cannot ignore, Papa."

"I thought as much. I believe your promised betrothal would need more time, my dear."

"Nonetheless, I come to beg you to change your mind in this instance. Please tell me that is so, Papa?"

"My dear, I do not agree with this notion of yours."

"What is the purpose behind the union, Papa? Why should I marry a man I do not love, nor is he ideal for me? He is much older than I am, and I fear we have not one thing in common. I feel no romantic attraction to him whatsoever. Please, Papa, I cannot marry him."

"My dear, listen to me. I have it on good authority that he would make a decent partner. He has a good reputation, and word is that he has by far all the wealth to support, not only you, my dear, but also all of your children. In these days of uncertainty, this is extremely important." He looked at his daughter with kindness as she sat opposite him on the sofa. "Please do not grieve so, my little one. You will see that you may be truly happy with the Count of Sussex. You must give him a chance to get to know you."

"Please, spare me, Papa. I do not wish to marry Count Leanard. He's insufferable. Furthermore, I have met someone, who, I do believe is a most excellent suitor, and whom you have briefly met on the night of the debut. Do you not remember the night of the ball and the young gentleman by the name of William? Could you not, at the very least, meet with him, please, Papa?"

Cruel Providence

"My dear, of course I shall. I will arrange a meeting for the day after tomorrow. I do not want to quarrel with my little princess, when all I desire is for her happiness. Nevertheless, you are young to the ways of the world. You must trust your Papa in regards to certain matters, especially in the financial world. I know many business matters that would only perplex you. Now, off you go." He gestured to Katherin kindly to take her leave. "But before you do, I will require the young man's family name."

"It is Mr. William Hampshire!" Katherin said with joy in her voice.

"Now off with you and please do not concern yourself with any affairs this evening, simply be happy, my child."

"Yes, Papa." Katherin exited the room with a grin on her face. Her accomplishments would finally enable her to marry the man who had taken her heart. She could not stop dreaming of him, his handsome face, strong stature and the kind twinkle in his eyes. For the first time in weeks, Katherin felt as though the floor underneath her feet was not collapsing beneath her.

Since Mr. Hampton was home with his family now, the following morning the children were again very excited at the prospect of spending time with him. They were all gathered at the breakfast table, when he announced that he had yet another surprise for them should they eat everything on their plates. They hurriedly devoured their breakfast before they sat quietly waiting for their father's surprise.

"Papa, won't you tell us please?" Genevieve, who could not wait any longer, interrupted her father's thoughts.

"Yes, yes. For the day I have a trip planned…"

"Oh, Papa, you are not going away yet again, are you?" Katherin shouted, sounding most alarmed.

"Now, please, Katherin, allow me to speak. If you please, today's trip will be for all of us to travel into town."

"Yes!" came a very jubilant loud cry of cheers from the children, who could hardly contain their excitement. Katherin was very pleased with this turn of events. She could not be happier.

They spent the whole day in town where their father bought many articles of clothing for each child. Again the children were so excited that they seemed to contaminate everyone with whom they came in contact. They encountered a variety of people, talking to the shop owners and tasting the delights offered by the many stores the family frequented. The children would point with astonishment; whence either Mr. Hampton or Katherin had to correct their manners. They returned to the estate exhausted, but nevertheless extremely pleased. It seemed a pity not to have more family outings, as this splendid day brought them closer together once again.

Chapter 9

The following day was filled with excitement, as Katherin knew she would have an encounter with Mr. Hampshire. Her dream of William the previous evening lasted the entire night, and unable to get him out of her mind, she could not wait to be in his presence. The morning was spent in good humour. The children had settled in their usual routine to Miss Louise's relief.

It was in the latter part of the afternoon when the door was answered, not to Mr. William Hampshire, but none other than the count himself. He came in to speak with Mr. Hampton. While they chatted in the study, Katherin came downstairs, wishing to find William after hearing voices in the corridors. She went to the study where she was dismayed to find the door closed. Katherin decided to stay close by for she would not want missing the dashing William again. She sat by the door for what seemed a long while, when at last, the study door opened.

"Oh, Count!" Katherin said, astonished.

"Miss Katherin, what a pleasure to have you sitting in waiting."

"No, I beg of you. I was not listening at the door, should you think me improper."

"I profess that I believe you are becoming very fond of me," the count went on to say while he grinned a wicked smile.

"I apologize, you have misunderstood!" Katherin uttered with desire to rectify the misunderstanding as quickly as she could, which was only too obvious to her, but regrettably not to him.

"My dear, as you know the count has come to court you for he has become very fond of you," Mr. Hampton said, looking proud as a peacock. Any father, in his position, would be so lucky as to have interested suitors, who would not only be good spirited, but also wealthy.

Katherin blushed profusely. While not wanting to quibble with her father in front of the count, she remained silent. She bowed her head before saying, "Father, may I have a word with you?"

The count looked as if he had been assaulted, for his demeanour quickly changed.

"Why yes, my dear girl," Mr. Hampton replied extending an arm for her to enter his study. They stood and fixed their gazes on each other. "Would you not be happy, since the count is very anxious to continue the courtship?" Mr. Hampton asked.

"Father, I was under the assumption that we agreed to meet with Mr. Hampshire. Why have you not spoken with him?"

"My dear, do not think ill of me, for I must tell you there were no replies from Mr. Hampshire. I have sent letters with not so much as a reply from him."

Katherin began to cry with tears falling onto her cheeks, stricken with a look of bewilderment on her face. "How could that be? I am extremely unsettled to hear this. Why would he not reply? I do not understand, Papa." she uttered, visibly distraught.

"I too am sorry. Therefore, I cannot refuse Count Leanard's offer to marry you," he added. Upon hearing this, Katherin ran out the door, up the stairs as quickly as she could, looking mortified.

"I must apologize, Count Leanard, for my daughter has suddenly taken ill."

"Make no apologies, Mr. Hampton. Conversely, I must make my own apologies. I had simply come for a stroll, yet I have much to organize in wedding preparations. Perhaps once I return from London, we could meet again. It seems a pity that young women say what they deem."

"Yes, I will have a word with Katherin, and I bid you good day, Count Leanard."

Afterward, Mr. Hampton sent for Katherin. She hesitantly met with her father. She unwillingly entered his study to see her father smoking his pipe while sitting comfortably in his leather chair with definite signs of fatigue. "You sent for me, Papa?" Katherin said nervously as she knew not what had been said after her outburst. Nonetheless, she was aware that it pertained to her earlier eruption.

"Yes, my dear. Please close the door. I must discuss some matters of great importance with you. I suspect that you think ill of the count and perhaps of me as well. I would like for you to reconsider the marriage proposal with the count. You must understand that there are many lives that will be affected by this marriage."

"Papa, I cannot reconsider, and to be quite honest, do you truly think I could be happy with someone I do not love? You do know how I feel. Therefore, I cannot imagine why you would want to pursue a man who I believe is insufferable." She deliberately voiced her strong objection.

"Why has he displeased you?"

"No, not in any un-gentlemanly manner. Yet, I cannot find myself spending an eternity with him either."

"Dearest, do not distress yourself. I have accepted his proposal regardless. He would like to see you before the wedding nuptials."

"What, Papa? How could you?" she shouted, and this time you could not mistake her outburst – Katherin was angry.

"I am very sorry to hear that you think ill of the count."

"However ill I think of him, you are convinced, and notwithstanding the fact, you insist on a marriage that totally disagrees with me! Perhaps had I not been more guarded with my affections for they lie undeniably elsewhere, you would be persuaded how strongly I am objecting to this ridiculous marriage."

"Before getting too crossed with me you must understand that it is with great regret that I cannot refuse the count's generous proposal. Do you not see that I am quite at a loss," Mr. Hampton flatly stated.

With these last words from her father, Katherin left the study in tears again. Mr. Hampton did not appear happy either, although distress would have his effect after their exchange.

The count had his rendezvous with Katherin as planned by her father. They had travelled to the count's residence for the afternoon. Her only thoughts were: *could this be the only suitable choice Papa has for me?* This day afforded her the opportunity to wear her lovely red dress, which she had great hopes to wear for William's eyes only. The idea of wearing such a beautiful gown to see the count was to taint it in blood – her own blood for she would rather die from a dagger wound then to be with someone she detested. It was dreadfully unfortunate that she could not persuade her father how unhappy she felt. She entered the count's drawing room where he was seated on a comfortable leather high-back chair crafted many decades ago for his grandfather most likely.

"Come closer, my dear, and do not be uneasy," the count said in a way that sent shivers up Katherin's spine.

"I can see you from a distance." Katherin attempted to ward off this unbearable man, who could not see that he was quite unwanted.

"I think not, my dear. You are not in your father's home where you can run away and hide in your chambers." A sinister smile erupted on his face that provoked more wicked shivers throughout her body.

The afternoon progressed in a most awkward fashion with little hope of Katherin escaping his long arms. They seemed to reach out like tree branches after shedding their leaves in autumn while his tentacle-like fingers wrapped themselves around her upper-arms. Katherin was only too pleased to return home where once again she could feel the safety of her family. How will she break free from this inescapable destiny with this man? She had no idea. She only felt the void in her heart accompanied of a strong urge to run away.

As Katherin entered the family foyer, her father was there to greet her that evening.

"My dear, how was your visit with your betrothed?"

"You may ask, though I believe you will not want to hear what I feel. Therefore, I find it pointless to speak." She expressed her feelings regardless of the outcome, while she felt no more could be lost since she had no voice in this particular affair.

"I am very distressed for your plight, my child, yet I have no recourse. I am deeply disturbed. I will ensure that the count promises to treat you with the highest regard," Mr. Hampton said.

"Papa, why can you not see how this causes me such misery?" Katherin again tried persuading her father to save her from a cruel fate. Where was her father's tenderness when it came to matters of the heart?

Chapter 10

The wedding was planned, though conceivably
Katherin was devastated to be marrying a man who
totally repulsed her. Her own father had pointed out
that many women marry men well established in
business, not unlike what she was to undertake.
Katherin spoke with her father only on necessary
occasions, since she was certain he would not listen to
her. She ate very little and this only reduced her
weight considerably in the weeks preceding the
wedding, while emphasizing a tinier waistline. Other
than leaving her room for short intervals for
necessities, Katherin remained in her bedchamber and
parlour where she continued to feel utterly miserable,
with no end in sight.

The wedding nuptials were to be held the
following day and while Katherin was unable to sleep
for fear of yet another nightmare, she rested very
little. During her dream state, she found herself in a
birdcage surrounded by many felines, who seemed
only too eager to consume her. Not able to relax, she
lay in her bed all night wondering how she would get
through the next day's ordeal.

How ever much she may have wished that the
morrow never came, the morning emerged after
unbearably long hours of darkness. Soon Miss Louise
entered Katherin's bedchamber, carrying a beautiful
white gown of satin and lace, which would have
brought much joy to the young maiden under any
other circumstance. Miss Louise helped Katherin with
her hair, styling it to a fashionable height adorned
with flowers while the maid entered the room to assist
her with the gown. After removing Katherin's

nightgown, to have her bathe, it was at that point that Miss Louise noticed how much weight Katherin had lost in the past while. She had to make last minute alterations for the gown to fit properly. Once Katherin was completely dressed by late morning, they turned Katherin around to view their creation.

"Oh my, Miss Katherin, you are quite stunning!"

Katherin was not conceited by any means. She did not have much vanity to feel that only the outer layers were a representation of the inner being.

"Thank you," she answered modestly.

"Child, you should be happy to marry such a fine gentleman. He is one who will be able to secure your future."

"I cannot feel equally pleased," Katherin said, showing her disapproval.

Her father escorted Katherin to the church in a regal coach, which he had hired for the occasion. He looked incredibly handsome himself dressed in his finest waistcoat, breeches, exquisite shoes and fine laced ruffled shirt, all of which had been tailored for him specifically for this occasion. He looked the dignified and a proud father he was.

In spite of this, Katherin wanted no part of today. Her demeanour reflected her inner feelings. She simply wanted to be spared of what should be her finest day. Her only thoughts were of Mr. William Hampshire, and how she would never see him again, since, from this day forth, she would only belong to another.

"Will you not be happy, my dear Katherin?" Mr. Hampton asked, wanting her to smile on her wedding day. He felt an ache in his heart when observing his little princess, who appeared ever so poignantly disappointed. However, he felt powerless to turn the event around to suit her needs and not the family's requirements.

"Papa, it grieves me to be walking down the aisle toward someone I simply abhor. I have not the faintest inclination to be with this man. You have condemned me to a life in his company. Therefore, you will understand when I say that I am very unhappy on this day and extremely disappointed with your decision." She had opened her heart and bore her resentful feelings to him. With no other reason than to contest this unreasonable marriage, she felt that if she stood any hopes of changing his mind, it was at this very instant.

"It pains me to hear your words, Katherin. You have made it quite clear that you would not accept the count. Unfortunately, you forget that women could not and will never have the opportunity to make an enormous decision such as marriage. So I pray you will forgive me, in time, and that you will put yourself at ease. There could be worse fate than to be with the Count of Sussex. He is not a dreadful man such as you seem to think. So it is for you to see the good in him, and when you do, your life may turn into one of exquisite delights and happiness. You must look at the bright side of this new chapter in your life. Life demands that you carry on even though you hold very strong views regarding this marriage. Therefore, my dear, make the best of it, will you not?" He looked at his gorgeous daughter once again before they would step into the church and walked slowly to the altar.

It was then that Katherin stopped her father and turned to him to say:

"Then, Papa, hear me out before it is too late. Are we simply property as cattle and shuttles to be disposed of? Are we not human beings who have dreams, and love to share with one another? To love and cherish one another, sharing what little time we have on earth with the one we treasure and desire, to prosper and have children, raising them with love and respect. Affection is not something that can be bought, but received such as you did with Mama. Can you not see this? Will you not admit that this marriage should not be so? Can you not stop this ridiculous charade before we are only left with regrets?"

Mr. Hampton shook his head. "You cannot understand the makings of the world at such a tender age. Should you have any grasp of the complexity of the business world, you would understand. So be happy, and you will soon discover that life can be good afresh. Now, please allow the wedding to begin," Mr. Hampton pleaded, taking his daughter's hand and placing it over his arm.

"But, Papa, you must understand that I cannot marry a gentleman with the kind of light in his eyes that does not conjure kindness and gentleness, and knowing that my heart would not race at the sight of him." Katherin had no other option but to tell it as it was. Obviously her father seemed deaf to hear her words of strong objections to wed.

In the end, the wedding proceeded with no other unenthusiastic incident. The church was decorated with white orchids interspersed with bluebells, and the atmosphere was one of celebration and endowment to enter a new episode in a young woman's life. Katherin did not smile once through the entire proceeding. Instead, she felt an intense dislike toward her new life. After the ritualistic verbal agreement between man and wife, a diamond tiara, adorned with a few flowers, was placed on Katherin's head. The Count of Sussex leaned in to kiss his new bride, but Katherin was utterly revolted although she stood still to allow him a simple kiss on the lips. Her father was displeased with how gloomily his daughter had behaved.

The reception that followed the church ceremony offered the numerous guests with plenty of food and drink. Katherin could not manage to eat at her own nuptial banquet, nor join in on partaking of the wine. At the end of the evening, Mr. Hampton came to Katherin to bid her farewell.

"My dear! Are you not ever to smile again?"

"No, Papa, I shan't!"

"I am very sorry to hear it. I had hoped you would come to realize what would be best for you, but unfortunately I suspect you have not."

"Papa, I do not want to stay here. Could I not return home with you?"

"I'm afraid not, child. You are presently a young married woman, and the count is your husband. You will have to abide by his rules from this day forth."

"Papa, please?" Katherin pleaded.

"I dare say it would please me enormously for you to give the count a chance to love you, and for you to do the same."

"Yes, Papa, only to please you!" she whispered with her head hung low.

Mr. Hampton took a step toward his daughter, lifted her head, and kissed her forehead, before making his exit with his family already waiting in the coach. He knew he was leaving his eldest daughter in a miserable state.

The count approached Katherin for them to say their farewells to their guests. Katherin was exhausted for sleep had not been possible during the past few days. The count touched her shoulder. Although Katherin retracted from his touch, Count Leanard appeared to be amused by her reaction, which entirely disturbed her.

"I am sorry you feel repulsed by my touch, then again you will have to get accustomed to it, for we are to spend a very long time in each other's company, my dear."

"You must give me time to adjust to my new surroundings. I am exhausted and wish to rest for I have not slept for the past few nights. Could I be excused?"

"Why yes, you may indeed, for I can wait to consummate our marriage another day, my dear."

Chapter 11

Katherin awoke to find herself in a very strange place. This was the first night she had not slept in her own bed. However, she would never have conceived to spend it in the count's house. Only in her worst nightmares would she have dreamt of this fate. She pulled the covers up to her chin not wanting to feel any more vulnerable than she had since meeting the count. Could this be her new reality? *Is this plausible?* She wished to close her eyes and find herself far from this hideous place she now must call home. While she hugged herself, she wished for her mother to tell her of what could come next. Katherin began crying when her eyes were already puffy from last evening's tears. She lay back down to cry herself to sleep.

A little while later, she awoke yet again but this time the servant girl was walking about her room. Once the maid saw she was awake, she drew the curtains open, allowing bright sunlight to penetrate the room. Katherin closed her eyes for the sheer brightness nearly blinded her already painful, swollen eyes. The servant noticing her mistress's distress, immediately drew the curtains closed. She then pulled the curtains slightly opened to allow Katherin's eyes to adjust to the bright sunlight.

"I am so very sorry, ma'am," she apologized, as though she would be whipped for such an improper, distasteful action.

"No, please! I am very sorry to have caused you distress. Please forgive me?" Katherin said, not wanting to cause anyone undue suffering.

The maid turned and lifted her head to give her mistress a small smile.

Katherin returned the smile for she desperately needed an ally. They were more or less the same age, whereas at the Hampton's residence, Katherin had servants much older than she was. They seemed to have found some common ground almost instantly. Having a friend would ease Katherin's pain. The girl appeared to be lovely as she had all the necessary qualities one finds in someone of the same age. Her hair was fashioned in a tight bun with a few brown curls on either sides of her face. She was a little heavier than Katherin, but not so that she may be carrying extra weight. She appeared to have carried out some heavy chores since her muscle tone depicted those of a hardworking young woman.

"Is everything all right, ma'am?" she asked, while looking at the swollen eyes that were staring right at her.

"I feel lost, that is all. I have not been away from home, nor left my family before this day," she said to the young maid who under any other circumstance could have become a close friend. "I am afraid I do not know your name, Miss...?

"Sorry, ma'am. My name is Mary." She again sounded apologetic.

"Thank you. Do you know what is expected of me this morning, Mary?"

"I'm afraid you have slept through the entire morning, ma'am. It was then that I was asked to assist you, for the count was concerned, I imagined, ma'am," Mary explained.

"Thank you, Miss Mary."

"No, ma'am please do not call me 'Miss Mary'. It is simply Mary, ma'am." She sounded distressed; her mistress calling her out of social order was unusual.

"Please excuse my lack of knowledge for I will address you as Mary then."

Katherin laughed for a second before she remembered where she was. How can she ever want to leave her bedchamber that was grand compared to the one she had at home. Could this be what she was born to do? She would never have conceived a destiny that was fraught with loveless people for she was brought up with the opposite. Then why would her father impose such a travesty on her?

After some precious time past in bathing and dressing, Katherin was about as ready as she would ever be to meet the man whose company she could barely tolerate. Although she wanted to please her father, she was not certain what the promise entailed. Perhaps if she merely had to hold hands, such as her parents did. Katherin felt it would not be unreasonable to ask for her to hold hands with the count. Therefore, she would be agreeable to do so, in spite of her strong feelings of distrust toward him. This suspicion was born out of a deep-seated feeling that she would find it hard to explain to others. She was optimistic regarding seeing the count however, for she hardly knew what he expected from her. She was quite naïve to the world of matrimony, which was limited to her parents holding hands and at best an innocent kiss.

Mary left Katherin in her room while another servant walked in to escort her to the count. He was waiting for his *little lamb* as though she were a prize horse in his stable.

"Countess, have you readied yourself to meet with the count?" the maid asked while she curtsied to Katherin.

"Who are you addressing in those terms?" Katherin glanced around the room for anyone who may have entered with the maid without her knowledge.

"It is you, Countess, the person I am addressing presently." She smiled at the look on Katherin's face. It was priceless.

"I thought you said 'Countess'. I do not see anyone other than myself and of course you in the room." Katherin sounded incredibly confused while continuing to gaze around the room.

"I am terribly sorry. You are the countess, ma'am. I assumed you knew," the maid blurted, wanting to laugh out loud.

"I am sorry, are you certain I am supposed to be addressed in this manner? For yesterday I was simply Miss Katherin Hampton." She was certainly bewildered. Katherin was far from conceiving that by marrying the count, she would earn the title.

"Yes, Miss Katherin, once you wed the count, you automatically became Countess of Sussex. You did not know?" She went on laughing for she had not ever heard of anyone so inexperienced.

Katherin blushed. "I am sorry that I amuse you so, but do forgive me for I am rather unaware of all the changes that have occurred in the past few weeks."

Katherin's life was changing at the speed of light and it reflected in her immaturity. Perhaps her father was right about not knowing the ways of the world.

"Do not worry yourself, Countess!" the maid said with the semblance of a smile on her face. "The count is waiting for you," she repeated.

"Yes, I believe you are correct. Would you care to take me to him?" Katherin asked. "I would not ask, but admittedly, I have not yet had a chance to visit the house properly."

"Yes, Countess," the maid answered.

"Thank you."

They both walked down a lengthy corridor adorned of elegant sconces hanging on the walls. They provided limited lighting. Katherin did not remember seeing this corridor before that day. *What a strange place,* she remarked to herself. Katherin was accustomed to a decorated dwelling, and not one of somewhat barren stones. To her, it felt cold and damp, quite unlike her family home, which was warm and cozy. The rich wood with which the family home had been decorated was a place that would forever remain in her memory.

The count was beginning to doubt whether Katherin would ever come down to the main dining hall. Just as he was prepared to send a third servant to fetch his new bride, Katherin finally appeared.

"Yes, Count," Katherin managed to say.

"That will be all." He motioned for the servant to leave them. The maid curtsied and left the two alone.

Katherin would have liked the servant to remain, but she knew that defying her husband would be the same as disregarding her own father's request.

"Did you sleep well, my dear?"

"Yes, thank you."

"Excellent, for we will journey out this day to stroll around the gardens. I look forward to viewing the marvellous grounds with you."

"That would be kind," Katherin had to agree.

Then she suddenly felt light-headed. She needed to eat or would soon feel faint. The count noticed her unexpected pallor.

"My dear! Please do sit to eat first, will you not?" The count was trying his best, obviously, to be a gentleman.

"That would be fine. Thank you."

She sat at one end of the table that could seat at the very least twelve people. There were fruit, loaves of bread, along with cheese laid out. The servant came in to fill their goblets with wine. Katherin ate a few grapes, some other fruits – she had to admit she was hungry – with a piece of bread and some flavourful cheese. She then sipped her wine quietly. She felt a little dizzy shortly afterward and realized that she should not have drunk the wine.

The count simply observed Katherin as she ate, making her quite uneasy. When he saw that she finished eating, he spoke. "It would be good to stroll before the weather takes a turn for the worst later today."

"Yes, that would be very nice indeed." Katherin needed to get out of this strange place.

They both stepped out after a warm wrap was placed over Katherin's shoulders. The wind was rather chilly, yet the sun was warm on her face. Admittedly, the grounds were spectacular, illustrating the beauty of the mid-spring flowers and the life that sprang from its darkened winter days. Some flowers were bursting their tender pink blossoms with their young leaves protruding from the bare branches. Katherin was in awe of the brilliant colours displayed in contrast to the lush green meadows. She had not seen so many species of plants where she grew up.

Her mother adored her rose garden. She had collected a variety of species through the years.

The count was pleased to see Katherin's reaction. It was very pleasing for he, too, enjoyed these gardens far too vast for a single man to appreciate alone.

"I must confess that I have many acres of land at my disposal. I have the largest piece of land in the county," he said, gloating somewhat.

"I agree it is beautiful," Katherin said.

"I would like for you to manage a little area in need of grooming, allowing you some useful duties should you feel fit for it," the count added. "At present, my dear, we must discuss other sleeping arrangements for the evening."

"What do you mean?" Katherin appeared startled.

Chapter 12

Mr. Hampton had been concerned about his daughter's marriage, as he personally knew very little of the Count of Sussex. On the other hand, Edward was assured by countless business acquaintances that the count was a respectable gentleman, possessing land and titles, but he knew little else about the man. He would have preferred a lengthy engagement rather than the short rushed one, which seemed to have been hastily organized by the count, who had in fact offered a sizeable endowment to marry Mr. Hampton's gorgeous daughter. It was customary for the father of the daughter to offer a dowry. In this case Katherin's dowry had been meagre; in exchange for which, Mr. Hampton stood to increase his wealth immensely with the marriage. Had the Hampton's estate been in a better financial position, he most likely would have prolonged the engagement, providing Katherin adequate time to mature, for then and only then she could have understood her duty with a man. Mr. Hampton was disturbed by the pleas she voiced during their last moments together. Her words rang endlessly in his mind after returning from the celebration. Perhaps the count did not have honourable intentions toward Katherin. Had he made the right decision? He hoped so, as he would not want to cause undue pain to his lovely princess. In the end his decision had secured him financially, while also securing young Edward's future. Land without funds was not an inheritance Mr. Hampton wanted to leave as a legacy to Edward. How ever secure this marriage had been, Mr. Hampton could not remove the haunting pleas from Katherin's last words before he walked her down the aisle. He could not rest easy.

The family life continued the same as usual nevertheless, at the dinner table, young Katherin's place was vacant for not only did Mr. Hampton notice, but the children also mentioned how they missed their sister.

Later that day and after knocking at Mr. Hampton's study, the governess entered his room. "Mr. Hampton may I enquire after Miss Katherin, that is Countess of Sussex?"

"Certainly."

"Have you heard any word from her before this day?"

"Not precisely, although we hope to hear by week's end," he added.

"I see. Did she appear happy once the ceremony had ended?"

"I'm afraid she was not."

"I had hoped she would recover her cheerfulness once the wedding was over. Perhaps the whole ordeal was overwhelming to her?"

"So did I," Mr. Hampton said, resigned to the fact that he sounded quite pleased with himself.

The governess curtsied before exiting the study.

Not long after she left him, he heard another knock, but this time it was at the front door. The butler answered the door.

A gentleman caller was shown into the study to speak with Mr. Hampton.

"Mr. Hampshire, sir," the butler announced.

Mr. William Hampshire stood in the doorway wanting to speak with the father of the love of his life.

"Do come in, Mr. Hampshire." Mr. Hampton indicated for the young man to sit down in one of the two high-back chairs opposite his desk. The study shelves displayed books, some of law that would be used in business, along with a huge fireplace mantel over which hung paintings of various members of the family. Among them was a painting of his strikingly beautiful wife, Constance.

"Thank you, sir," William Hampshire answered, taking a seat.

"What brings you here, and what can I possibly do for you, Mr. Hampshire, since I have not heard any replies from the letters I sent to you?"

"I had made great efforts to be here earlier this week, although I have been unforeseeably detained. I have come to ask for your daughter's hand in marriage, Mr. Hampton."

"I'm afraid you are too late, Mr. Hampshire."

"But, sir, how can that be?" William protested. He appeared grief-stricken.

"I'm afraid she has pronounced her vows only a few days ago. When you failed to show, the wedding proceeded, for the count was most anxious to wed."

"I did not know that one day would be detrimental to meeting with you, Mr. Hampton. My detainment was totally unexpected for I believe it was most likely due to preventing the engagement between Miss Katherin and me!" William said, quite distressed.

"I am sorry on how the events proceeded, sir, then again my daughter's concerns are no longer in my control. Count Leanard is the sole owner of her hand, and as you may have heard, he is a very powerful man in these parts. You do understand?"

"I cannot believe this ill-fated turn of events. I shall not be deterred, Mr. Hampton. I believe the count has had a hand in these thwarted events and I shall get to the bottom of it. You can be assured of it."

Cruel Providence

William angrily rose to leave. He bowed, took a few paces to exit the study before stopping briefly to retrieve his cloak and cane from the butler. The manservant opened the front door for Mr. Hampshire to exit the house. He climbed into his carriage and disappeared quickly around the corner.

Mr. Hampton shook his head and was somewhat confused as to what had just transpired.

"Wilkes!" He called out for the butler.

"Yes, sir."

"Can you ready the carriage? I am in mind to seek news in regards to what has happened to Mr. Hampshire," Mr. Hampton told him.

"Yes, sir." Wilkes exited the residence to order the stable boy to ready the carriage. Mr. Hampton then ran up the staircase to ready himself while informing the governess of his intended absence. He descended the stairs, quickly grabbed his topcoat, and left the house. He climbed into his carriage and ordered the driver to take him to town.

Miss Louise was taken aback by Mr. Hampton's sudden departure. Mr. Hampton had not mentioned the trip when she had spoken with him only half-an-hour ago. Could there be an emergency with Miss Katherin … that is Countess Katherin? Only such an event would have created the change in Mr. Hampton's plans. She could only wonder what took place. The children were waiting for Miss Louise inside their study room.

"Did Papa want to surprise us, Miss Louise?" Genevieve asked.

"I am not certain, children. We must concentrate on the task at hand, thus we will read from the storybook," Miss Louise said, sitting down again.

Mr. Hampton arrived in town where he entered his gentlemen's club. Many of his business associates were seated discussing matters of politics and trade while drinking some liquor or wine. The air was filled with good humour and sounds of passionate discussions.

"Ah, Mr. Hampton! What brings you into town so soon after your daughter's wedding?" Mr. Murray asked. Mr. Murray had been a good friend of Edward for many years.

"I would like to find answers to a few pressing questions," he stated.

"Do sit down and join us then." Mr. Murray pointed to the empty chair at his table. He was a robust man wearing a gorgeous wig and a smile that one could hardly resist.

"I most certainly will as soon as I speak with the gentleman seated over the far side of the room, and I will return shortly."

Mr. Hampton walked toward an acquaintance of the count to question him regarding his knowledge of the count's intentions toward his daughter.

"Mr. Jenkins. May I have a word with you, in private?"

"Certainly." Mr. Jenkins stood up, and walked out into the hall for a private chat with Mr. Hampton. "What can I do for you, Mr. Hampton?"

"You are a good acquaintance of the Count of Sussex, are you not?"

"Why yes, although it is not news, Mr. Hampton." He sounded confused. Mr. Jenkins was near the same stature as Edward.

"It has come to my attention that the count possibly caused an injustice. Have you heard, or have you any knowledge of his wrong doing with regards to marrying my daughter?" Mr. Hampton went on showing his apprehension while peering into Mr. Jenkins's steady gaze.

"I cannot say that I have heard of any wrongful injustice, Mr. Hampton," Mr. Jenkins replied, becoming more alarmed; wondering where these questions were headed.

"Should you become aware of any information; would you be so kind as to alert me?" Mr. Hampton was well aware that he questioned Mr. Jenkins regarding his loyalty toward the count. At this point, he did not much care. His daughter's welfare was at stake. He could feel it.

"Yes, certainly."

"Thank you, Mr. Jenkins."

Mr. Hampton then bowed and turned to return to the gentlemen at the table seated with Mr. Murray.

"Mr. Hampton, do join us would you, please?"

"Yes, yes," Mr. Hampton replied, taking a seat across from Mr. Murray.

"Did you find what you came for?" Mr. Murray asked.

"Not entirely," Mr. Hampton said, quite agitated.

"Now, old boy, what on God's earth has you so distressed soon after your daughter's wedding? I would have thought you would be celebrating her taking her vows. I dare say he seems to be quite the catch, even for your daughter. The count has kept to himself after the death of his first wife however, and unfortunately, little has been known of him since."

"I was not aware of the count losing his first wife. Did you hear of how she died?' Mr. Hampton queried, now sounding most anxious with more uneasiness in his demeanour.

"I'm afraid not, Edward."

"I have a notion to visit the count," Mr. Hampton stated.

"What the devil for? They are likely enjoying their honeymoon."

"Simply to see for myself how happy young Katherin is."

"I understand perfectly well, yet do you not consider that both the count and Miss Katherin would be blissfully enjoying themselves?" Mr. Murray asked, smiling. "And perhaps not desirous of your company at this point?"

"Yes, nevertheless, I must ensure her safety. I thank you, but I must leave. I do have a few errands to run before returning."

"Of course. You must not become a stranger then," Mr. Murray added before Mr. Hampton left the table to exit the club.

Mr. Hampton then rose, bowed and took his leave rather hurriedly.

He carried out his necessary errands while questioning many businessmen regarding the possibility that the count had caused some unkindness towards his family. However, he did not uncover any evidence of what Mr. Hampshire had advanced only a few hours ago. He then deduced that Mr. Hampshire may have been mistaken.

Chapter 13

They had strolled for what seemed an excessively long time as Katherin shivered from the cold. The count had been so engrossed in his pleasure of showing his garden to his new wife that he failed to notice the cold wind. However when he finally noticed her shivering, he decided to invite her back into the mansion. They entered into the foyer and proceeded across to the drawing room where a raging fire in the hearth of the fireplace was warming the entire room. Katherin was only too delighted to be near the fire and warming her hands. She soon felt much better. The spring weather was still cool at times, and today one could still feel the chill in the air. The count then excused himself for a few moments to return at Katherin's side only minutes later.

"I have taken the liberty to bring you some warm milk, my dear. I hope it is to your liking," he stated.

"Thank you," Katherin answered, taking the tumbler from the count's hands.

"May I bring you some bread and cheese as well?" Apparently Count Leanard was making great strides to accommodate his bride.

"No, that is quite fine. I thank you," Katherin replied. She was beginning to wonder whether she had mistaken her fears for a misplaced apprehension of being married to an older man. She also questioned if being married was very different to what she was used to at home. Here she seemed to be treated with attentive gestures and kindness. If one could ignore the fact that her family were nowhere in sight, this situation appeared to be similar to what she found at her father's home. Perhaps she could resign herself to becoming accustomed to the daily routines of the mansion, along with being a married woman. She sighed with that last thought.

Katherin sat in the oversized armchair across from the count, who had taken a seat in the identical chair. They both gazed into the fire. The flame seemed to have mesmerized them for they did not speak for a long while. Katherin felt self-conscious should his lordship turn his gaze to her. He, in turn could not refrain from throwing her a glance from time to time. After several long minutes of silence, he turned his attention upward to the portrait of his grandfather, which hung above the fireplace.

"He was a great man, my grandfather that is!" he pointed out while gazing at the portrait.

"I am sure he was. He appears to be a very proud man in the manner in which he stands," Katherin noted with a faint smile drawing on her lips.

"You would have admired him as everyone who knew him did, Countess."

Katherin had not heard the count address her in such a way. She stared at him in shock as though he had called her something unpleasant.

"Oh yes, of course," she finally answered after a moment of speechlessness.

"I would like to speak to you regarding our sleeping arrangements for this evening," his lordship said.

"What have you in mind, sir?" she replied, not wanting to acknowledge where the conversation was headed.

"The fact that we are married affords for a husband to sleep with his wife occasionally. You do understand this is practiced in all of society. Had your father not slept with your mother?" the Count asked, hoping to receive a positive reply.

"Of course they had, but mostly they had separate bedchambers," Katherin admitted.

"I would have it no other way for our marriage."

"I…, I…" she stammered.

"No, it is agreeable for a woman to be modest, perhaps a little timid at the beginning of any marriage. I would doubt that, in your virginity, should you be otherwise," he reassured Katherin; her fears being quite natural.

"Of course. Could I beg your forgiveness? I am not certain I may be able to accommodate your wishes at the present moment, Count," she said.

Her life was changing so fast that it was difficult to keep up with the swift pace.

"Do not concern yourself at the moment. In time, we will adjust to our new life."

"I must admit that I would prefer my life to remain as it is. I do fear your presence, sir." Katherin sighed inaudibly. She had finally admitted to his lordship her innermost dread, for it had gripped her and it was becoming increasingly difficult to restrain the turmoil within.

"Not to worry, my dear. We will discuss this later. Presently, would you be so kind as to relax, and dine with me? Dinner will be served shortly."

Katherin had only time to offer a nod in response to the count's query when a sudden knock came at the door. "Yes," the Count called out.

The butler entered, announcing, "Mr. Edward Hampton, to see your lordship."

"Yes, of course. Show Mr. Hampton in, would you?"

As Edward Hampton entered the parlour, the count stood up and turned to him. Katherin, in the meantime was stunned – and very pleased to see her father. *Finally!*

"Ah! Mr. Hampton, how good of you to come. How are you this fine day?"

"Count, it is nice to be here so soon after your nuptials. Do forgive my intrusion." Mr. Hampton was rather curt with his responses it seemed.

"Not at all. Do come in, and please have a seat," Count Leanard said, indicating a third seat beside him and facing the fireplace.

"Thank you," Mr. Hampton said.

He was delighted for the fire was a welcome sight – and imparted warmth for which he was grateful. The day had turned quite overcast and the wind was sweeping over the land mercilessly. At a glance, he could see for himself that his princess was smiling at his presence. Katherin's eyes fell onto her father.

"Katherin you look beautiful, child," Mr. Hampton told her, finally addressing his daughter.

"Thank you, Papa. I am very pleased of your visit," she said, a broad smile drawing on her lips. You could not discount her feeling of relief as well.

The count observed both Katherin and her father's interaction. He noticed how young Katherin behaved with him. Perhaps, he should have delayed their marriage until she was sufficiently mature to accept her fate. Needless to say, the count felt he would not wait for such an exquisite beauty to escape his grasp, as the competition had become fierce and would only increase with time. Her youthful beauty would only blossom with age.

"May we ask the reason for your visit, Mr. Hampton?" his lordship queried.

"Yes, of course. I was wondering whether we could have a word in private." Mr. Hampton sounded insistent.

"Of course." He turned to his wife. "Katherin, would you leave us for a short moment?"

She stood up and curtsied before leaving the parlour.

Once Katherin left, Mr. Hampton questioned the count about his intentions toward his daughter in a most subtle manner. Both men were not aware of Katherin's presence by the door. She knew it was unladylike to listen at doors, nevertheless, she felt it necessary to know the reason for her father's unexpected visit. She desperately wanted to know what brought him all the way from their country home on such a cool spring evening.

She listened intently. She thought she heard her father accuse his lordship of some kind of improprieties. She was not entirely sure as to what they might be. She pressed her ear to the door, but still, it was difficult to hear what the count's retort was to the accusations. No doubt, he was desperate to persuade her father otherwise, despite the fact that she had not heard what was distressing her father.

Mr. Hampton and the count had words, but unfortunately Katherin could not overhear. What she did hear however was, "if you have been up to anything untoward, I will find out!" Mr. Hampton said, before leaving his lordship's presence. He walked angrily to the door. Upon hearing footsteps, Katherin removed herself from the doorway. She would have been mortified to have been caught eavesdropping on their conversation. She immediately ran up the stairs only to descend the steps, pretending to come down to bid her father goodbye.

"Oh, Papa, are you to leave so soon?" she asked, wishing he would stay a while longer.

"I'm afraid so. I will not be able to remain, my dear." He then leaned in to embrace her, saying in a whisper, "I will be back for I am not going to leave you."

"What do you mean, Father?"

"I will explain soon. However, for now you only need to know that I will be returning. Do you hear me?" he added in a murmur, leaving Katherin nonplussed.

Katherin was left dazed by what transpired a minute ago, and she knew not why her father had gone so soon, and very shortly after their wedding. She knocked at the door.

"Yes, do come in," an irritated shout rang out from the count.

"Very sorry to interrupt. I was wondering why my father left so suddenly? I thought that perhaps he would remain to visit with us." Katherin attempted to question the bizarre incident that occurred minutes ago.

"My dear, do not concern yourself with trivial matters. Gentlemen are certainly able to take care and look after one young lady such as yourself, do you not concur?" He turned the question back to her, knowing that Katherin would not challenge his inequitable remark.

"Perhaps so, Count Leanard," she admitted however. She knew that something was in the offing. It was most likely she who would have to discover what the matter was.

"Would you care to have dinner now, my dear? We will be journeying out early in the morning, and we may not have the proper time to eat once we set off."

"Why yes, that would be kind," Katherin replied, rather enthusiastically. The meal would provide her with ample time to address his lordship regarding the matter in hand – her father's visit.

The count rose from his chair, walked across the floor to give his order for dinner.

A long time passed before he returned. Katherin took the opportunity of finding herself alone to try comprehending what could be so disturbing as to bring her father out for a short yet stormy visit.

"Is all fine?" she asked his lordship once he returned.

"Oh yes, my dear," he replied with undue concern as to what had come to pass between him and her father.

Although Katherin did not feel that all was in good order, especially with the odd circumstance surrounding her father's hurried departure and the comments he whispered into her ear, she tried to calm down just the same.

The servant soon came in with a tray of poultry garnished with spring vegetables, which he placed in front of the count. The maids then came in with cheese and a loaf of bread, while the sommelier brought in the wine.

The count stood up, carved the chicken and deposited a piece of white meat in Katherin's plate while the servant spooned some vegetables beside it.

As soon as they were left alone, and before he began eating, his lordship said, "There, my dear, eat to your heart's content. Afterward we will rest for a while before we retire. Tomorrow I have planned a small surprise for you. Thereby the reason for our early morning rise."

The count then started eating. He threw Katherin a rather mocking smile from time to time. The strange look on his face was disquieting to Katherin. The smiles he had been giving her earlier that day were genuine; this one, however, was not.

"I did not know you had planned such an outing for the following day. Was this why my father has come for a visit?"

"It does seem that nothing can escape your notice, Countess!" he said.

Then again she had not felt it was a compliment but intended the remark at her simple-mindedness.

The food was most delicious. Katherin hadn't eaten much for what seemed days, especially the week leading to the wedding. After the meal, it was apparent that his lordship desired to bed Katherin as he touched her hand and reached up, touching her arm. Katherin recoiled slightly from his show of affection however. She managed to stop before she had totally withdrawn, so as not to insult him. How ever noble her efforts had been, his lordship gave Katherin the most dreadful glare, which only served to frighten her. She even began to think that she had been foolish to believe for one moment that the count had her best interest at heart. She knew that she was fearful for a reason, and yet she had let her guard down for the past twenty-four hours. Could her first instincts be correct? Perhaps before long, she would find the answer to more questions.

"My dear, Katherin! You are now at the beck-and-call of your husband. You are my wife. Should you recoil once more from my touch, I will certainly react in a way that you would have good reasons to recoil. Do I make myself clear, my dear?" His lordship had made his feelings very clear indeed!

Judging from his intense glowering gaze, Katherin knew that he was serious. This terrified her to the point of being speechless, her mouth agape from sudden fright. She honestly knew nothing like the dread that overtook her. Not one person had ever upset her in such a way.

The count took Katherin's hand again, pulled her up to her feet and drew her into his embrace before kissing her hard on the lips. Katherin initially struggled to free herself, however, she proved to be no match for his manly strength. She gave up her struggle for she realized he would do as he pleased with her. She could do nothing to change the outcome. Even her father had come today and had appeared to have left defeated in his purpose. She soon realized that her existence was to become one of fright and anxiety. Nothing could have prepared her for what to do next. She had definitely not been instructed in these areas that proved to be more than her innocent life had instructed. She simply pushed away once the count thought she was not reacting to his advances.

His lordship peered into her eyes, probably wondering what she was thinking. Katherin was certain that he could not readily comprehend her reaction. He subsequently did the oddest thing; he walked towards the foyer and turned to her saying: "I will expect you will be ready soon for I shall consummate our marriage within the time that I have granted you!"

He then left her standing alone in the room. She did not know what would be expected of her. It was clear that her husband was terribly angry with her. His fierce gaze indicated that he perhaps found her intolerable.

Frozen with fear, Katherin lingered for a long time before she managed to move. She then decided to tiptoe up the stairs to return to the sanctuary of her bedchamber. She felt as if every step was the last one she would take. The sound of the creaking wood under her feet increased her dread. She could not think how she would escape her destiny.

With the assistance of her chamber maid, she undressed, donned her night gown while shivering from fright. A few moments later the maid came in to stoke the fire for the night. She placed a hot-water bottle under the blanket, curtsied and then asked if Madam would need her anymore tonight.

Katherin told her that she would not be needed today and slipped under the covers in order to stay as warm as possible. Sleep did not come easy for Katherin however, as she lay in bed for hours with gripping terror while clutching her covers tightly to her chin. Could this be her life from this point on? For some strange reason, she expected a little more from it. Moreover, she wondered what her father had come to discuss with her husband. And then he had left without as much as a clear explanation. *How could Papa do such a thing?*

Chapter 14

William Hampshire was so filled with rage after his encounter with Mr. Hampton that he was overwrought with anger and turmoil. His jaw was tense; brows furrowed, and stressed as he was, he became insufferable for those around him. His good companion, Mr. Franklin Shelby could not appease William. At the very least, he made efforts to hear his friend. They both discussed the marriage of the woman for whom he had the best intentions to do right, and who had captivated his heart the moment he laid eyes on her beautiful face. Now it looked as though he had lost her forever with the unforeseen turn of events. And since that instance, it would not provide satisfaction, or sleep, while her image danced in his mind and would not escape him as though there was a pre-set destiny associated with her. Fate would afford him no peace until he married her, until he had her in his arms, and could embrace her tenderly.

"There must be a way to obtain information, and thus annul this marriage," Frank said. "Perhaps it is not too late."

"I do not know how we could liberate her from the clutches of this insufferable demon for she is to be guarded by many within the estate, day and night I would imagine. What's more she would be kept under the watchful eye of the count." William could not be more miserable.

"We shall have a plan, a disguise of course, to free her. Do not be distressed, William. We both must call for skilful strategy to rescue her," Frank said, trying to calm his best friend.

The best the two men could hope for at this point was to plan Katherin safe rescue diligently and secretly, resulting in her return home to her father.

"Perhaps we could gain admission as delivery workers?" Frank suggested.

"Better still, we gain entry as members of Miss Katherin's relatives visiting from afar, who by no fault of our own were detained before the wedding ceremony," William countered. "This, of course, would not bring suspicion to anyone's mind since the wedding was hastily performed."

"That is a much better suggestion. We could gain access to the main parlour where surely Miss Katherin would be," Frank agreed.

For the first time, William was excited at the prospect of rescuing his beloved from the clutches of the Count of Sussex.

By late evening they came to an agreement as to their plan for rescuing Katherin from whom William believed was an evil man. It had been too late in the day to visit his lordship for he surely would consider their late call as unwarranted. And, assuredly, they could not afford any amount of distrust on the part of the count. Therefore, William had another tormented and sleepless night, where he would not know whether his love was safe from his lordship. Incomprehensible as it seemed; by some devious scheme his lordship had persuaded Katherin's father to let him have her hand in marriage. William could not fathom what his lordship had had to offer Mr. Hampton to allow the marriage to take place. Could there be more deceit than first thought or perhaps some measure of desperation? For him to hand over Katherin to a man such as Count of Sussex, who, amongst other things, was twice her age, was far from understandable. *What could it be?* He could not believe that after finally finding the woman who he had repeatedly seen in his dreams, he lost her to that wretched man. William had taking a strong dislike of the count. Sleep came very late, only in the early hours of the morning. He could not quiet his mind as his thoughts and feelings of anger, disgust, and concern for Miss Katherin jostled for first place in tormenting him. Katherin, according to him, was clearly wedded to the wrong man.

By early morning, the two men had disguised themselves to continue with their mission. They both took care to use every precaution to rescue their damsel in distress, for their youthful minds imagined all possibilities. The men took two good horses, and rode in a carriage in disguised fashion as to better convince the count of their genuine relationship with Katherin. The goal was to be relatives arriving from afar. The journey took over an hour, although William felt it had been much longer. During the journey, he became distraught for not arriving on time to prevent the wedding, and saving her from what must be the most undesirable fate imaginable. He imaged his lordship touching her and this only fuelled his anger. He was convinced that the count had deliberately devised a malevolent plan to detain him from his dutiful purpose of speaking with Mr. Hampton.

Frank had been looking out of the carriage window when he finally turned to William, and saw how anxious his friend appeared to be.

"William, you must remain calm, for the undertaking depends entirely on your attitude."

They went over both their plans in great detail. In the event that the first plan did not afford them a victory, surely the second scheme would be successful.

As soon as they arrived, both were escorted to the main entrance, where they were received by the major d'homme and their presence announced as cousins of the Countess Katherin of Sussex.

The butler came to meet the two men in the foyer only to pass on the message that the Count and Countess of Sussex had departed for parts unknown a few hours earlier.

Chapter 15

The count had left with Katherin an hour earlier than previously arranged. He had felt a strong urge to leave as soon as possible. There was no reason to delay, and since his lordship had not slept, it therefore made sense to him to wake Katherin before daybreak.

Katherin had been fast asleep, when Mary entered her room holding a lit table chandelier. She was sent to help Katherin in getting ready for her long excursion. Katherin was so sleepy that she rose with great effort. Mary was extremely pushy compared to the demeanour she presented the previous day. After Katherin had dressed in her woollen day gown, Mary aided her to put on a warm coat, mitts, and hat.

To show her gratitude to Mary, Katherin embraced the girl. Mary was shocked. She was not used to such displays of affection from her mistress. She had no clue on how to accept an embrace.

"Thank you, Mary, for your assistance," Katherin said after releasing her.

"Countess, you are quite welcome," Mary replied, still in disbelief. "We must hurry to meet the count, milady. He will be most anxious to leave."

Katherin could not imagine what kind of emergency could necessitate such an early rise. "Why should any journey be started so very early?" Katherin wondered out loud.

Mary ignored her remark and hastily assisted her mistress down the stairs to the waiting carriage parked in the front entrance where his lordship was being quite impatient.

The count sighed heavily, saying, "That is good. We must leave at once. We will not reach our destination this day. Could we manage to climb in the coach a little quicker for we must not be detained longer than we have already?" he complained.

Katherin could only imagine that once men became older, they grew ever more temperamental.

"Yes, I am in." She then turned to her maid. "Thank you, Mary, for all your help." Katherin smiled at her while ignoring her husband's impatience and bad temper.

Katherin noticed once again that Mary seemed different this day, for she reacted with coldness of heart. She could not imagine why she showed such a callous behaviour. Katherin did notice, however, that the count threw the poor girl a scornful glance. Perhaps he was the cause of Mary's change of attitude.

His lordship sat opposite Katherin before he shouted to the driver to drive on.

"Yes, milord," was the driver's simple reply.

"Why must we leave before sunrise?" Katherin asked.

"Why delay? Besides we must arrive before we miss our rendezvous," was the only explanation the count offered. "You might want to show less amity towards the servants," the count remarked. He seemed averse to Katherin showing any sign of affection toward anyone except him.

They rode for what seemed hours while they both sat without further words. The latter part of their journey was spent sleeping, as the trip proved to be long and tiring. Nodding to sleep such as Katherin did, was a nice reprieve from the tension she had felt within the coach. When they, at last, arrived in the village, Katherin woke from her slumber. She glanced around her for she did not recognize her location in any particular fashion.

"Where exactly are we?" she queried.

The count did not reply, but simply descended the few steps off the carriage, and walked toward to a gentleman standing by the inn's entrance. They exchanged a few words, which Katherin could not hear. His lordship then proceeded inside the inn for a few moments while Katherin continued to look around her through the carriage's window. The people she could see seemed to be in some hurry for some unfathomable reason. It must be the practice in other towns to be running about, for where she came from, no one appeared to be in such haste.

The count came out of the inn and walked towards the carriage. "Well, my dear, this is where we will disembark," he declared rather nonchalantly.

"What do you mean?" she said, sounding baffled.

"I will explain once we are inside," he replied, extending a hand to help her down the carriage's steps.

"I don't understand?"

"Come with me," he demanded.

"Yes, of course," she replied, feeling confused, not to mention how scared she felt. They both entered the inn. A servant girl greeted Katherin with a curtsy, and instantly took the small bag that Mary quickly packed that morning.

The count said, "You will wait here in the room that Mr. Blithe has kindly arranged for you. I must continue the journey without you for the time being. It is very late and the journey took far longer than originally planned. The roads are quite impassable in some areas that our journey will be delayed should we take the coach. Besides you will be more comfortable here."

After looking around the dark inn, Katherin felt alarmed at what she saw. "I still do not understand what this is concerning. Please, your lordship, I do not wish to stay here!" She truly sounded distressed.

"Not to worry, my dear. You will be safe here until I return." His words did not sound genuine.

"Why will you not take me?"

"At the present time, it is too dangerous and as I have mentioned, the roads are impassable. I don't think you wish to ride on horseback, do you?"

Katherin shook her head and raised her gaze to her husband. "Then why not send me back, or better still, tell the carriage driver to take me back to my father's home?" She sounded fearful.

"No!" came his only reply. The count was beginning to lose his temper by this time. He had a frightening temper and one never knew when it would surface and terrorize the people around him. Katherin had not encountered such stern behaviour before meeting and marrying the count.

The servant escorted the countess to her room. At the very least, the inn was warm. Katherin was handed her bag before the servant curtsied and then turned to exit. Katherin was left alone in a strange place without anyone to attend to her needs. What bothered her was that she did not have any knowledge as to when the count would return. How long she would have to remain in this small room, she knew not.

She sat on the bed where she began crying. She could not understand how her world had turned into a true mystery. One day she felt happily secure with her family, and the very next, she was traveling with her husband to God only knew where. She had dreamt of adventures, but this was beyond any of her imaginings.

After a good cry, Katherin cleaned her face, deciding to venture out. Hunger pains had overcome her desire to remain safe in her room. She opened the door slightly at first to see if anyone that may pose a threat was lurking about the corridor. When she saw no one, she proceeded down the stairs in search for some fruit perhaps. As Katherin stepped off the last step however, she came face to face with a man who propositioned her to go back to his room.

"I have never and will not be treated with such disregard, sir. And do remove your hand from my arm this instant," she demanded.

"Well, well look what we's got here?"

"Sir, let go of me!" she ordered once again.

"You, sir will let go of the lady?" Katherin heard a male voice speak forcefully at them.

"I was talking to the lady," the first man said. He had grabbed her arm but released it now with a smirk on his lips. He went up the stairs, at last leaving Katherin alone.

"Thank you, sir," Katherin said to the stranger, with some relief.

"Are you hurt?"

"No, not at all."

"Are you alone then?" he went on asking.

"For a short time, sir," she replied, not wanting to give too much information for fear of unwanted attention, especially after what happened moments ago.

"I am also remaining over night, but I must be traveling early the next morn."

"Yes, I shall be leaving very shortly as well. But for now, please excuse me, I must find the innkeeper or publican." Katherin then turned before she went around the corner to the counter facing the bar.

"Yes, sir, could I trouble you for some food and beverage," she asked the burly man behind the counter. "The count did not leave me with any indication as to where I could sit to eat an evening meal."

"Why yes, Countess, we can fix you a dish. Would you like it in your room?" he asked.

"Yes, that would be excellent," she replied.

Katherin decided that it was likely safer to remain in her room from now on end. She then went back to her room and waited for the maid to bring her meal to her. When she heard a knock at the door, Katherin went to open it only to find the servant girl with a platter standing in the embrasure.

"Thank you. I am famished. We left in such haste that we did not have a meal earlier in the day," she said to the young maid. She set the tray on the scanty looking dresser, and then left Katherin to herself.

Katherin ate, finally enjoying the stew, bread and cheese; although she had tasted better meals than this one. She couldn't think of what she could do next while waiting for the count's return. She read for a while – a book which she had brought with her in her luggage. When she lay down, it wasn't long before she was fast asleep. She must have dreamt of William, who was speaking with her, asking her to dance. She heard the door open wondering why they were being interrupted while they danced to the beautifully composed music of an Allemande. She was suddenly grabbed with one hand on her mouth and the other around her arm, twisting it behind her back.

"Do not make a sound for you shall die!" was the man's direct order.

"I beg your pardon?" she called out while startled out of her slumber.

Her words were garbled since the man's grubby hand was placed over her mouth.

"Not a word!" he repeated. "You will come with me for I will take you to see the count."

"What do you mean? Where is the count?" Katherin whispered through his fingers not certain what was really happening at this moment.

"Not another word and do not worry, miss," was his simple reply.

She was escorted down the stairs, exiting through the side door. So frightened Katherin was, she did not dare object to his instructions.

Chapter 16

William Hampshire was most distraught when he received word that the count took Katherin away. Once again, he was too late. Frank could see his friend's anguish, and his obvious resignation of having failed yet again. Frank was a man who was shorter in stature than William, but handsome enough. He had dark hair with a narrow moustache. He was broad shouldered. His Roman nose was strong and gave his face a god-like appearance. He was brave but not daft not to know when he was defeated.

"We will find her, I promise you. Let me have a word with the servants for they surely must know where his lordship took her. And do not worry, William," Frank said as he turned to the door again.

"Yes," William said, lifting his defeated gaze to Frank. All he could do was to sit in the carriage while Frank questioned the count's servants.

Frank soon came out – a smile on his lips.

"Great news! The count is headed south. We will move in that general direction, and question any one who may have seen them. I am sure we will find them. They have left but a few hours ago. Therefore, it would be best to leave the carriage behind, for riding horses will certainly gain speed."

"Yes, that is a good suggestion, Frank. I do not know what I would have done without you," William replied, a glimmer of hope lighting his face.

They rode as quickly as possible while not wanting to exhaust the horses for they did not know where the end of the road might be. The morning was quite chilly which made it for a better ride for the horses.

Cruel Providence

They arrived at a small hamlet, and decided to stop to ask anyone if they had seen a carriage, carrying the Count of Sussex, come through these parts. William had words with a shopkeeper, and then a servant, but neither of them had seen a carriage pass through. William now doubted whether they were travelling in the right direction. While William went inside a publican's establishment to purchase a drink of ale, Frank headed to the stables to ask the livery attendant if anyone had asked for fresh horses or left a carriage in his care. The stable boy said he witnessed a carriage come through right about dawn, for he thought it odd to see travelers before first light. Frank returned where the horses were tethered, waiting for William to return.

"Yes, William, I did speak to a young lad who by chance saw a carriage at dawn, driving past he did!" Frank sounded quite excited to impart the news to his friend for he had not seen William smile in the last few days.

"That would be them, I can only suppose," William agreed. "Perhaps we will continue another mile or two, as we cannot be too far behind."

"Yes, there is little hope but hope there is," Frank agreed.

They both rode off with renewed vigour, for finding Katherin before too long was now probable.

At long last they arrived in a village. By then, it was late afternoon and the sun was already setting in the evening sky. Once again, they walked around town to see whether a carriage had come through these parts. William went to the inn first.

"Pardon me, sir," he asked the publican, "Have you seen a coach carrying a lady and a gentleman pass through this fine morn or afternoon?"

"Why yes, sir. There were two such travelers, but they stopped," the publican informed William.

"Are they still here then?"

"No, sir, the gentleman left the lady for the night, but she was gone when the servant went to collect her tray. Not sure where she has gone though."

"By any chance would you have a suggestion as to where she might have gone?" William asked. He had nothing to lose.

"No, she simply left, disappeared without a word."

"Thank you for your assistance." William handed the man a coin for his troubles before turning around to leave. He then rejoined his friend to relay the information. It was his only lead in locating Katherin.

They were not certain as to what they were to do next however. They did not know what direction Katherin would have taken and who was in her company if the count was not with her. They decided to spend a little time in the village. Someone might have seen her leave the inn or walk about the village's lanes.

Frank passed by the livery stables to ask around, whereas William walked to the shop across the street.

"Ma'am, sorry to bother you?" William said as he entered the shop.

"Yes, sir. What can I fetch you?" she asked with a pleasant smile adorning her wholesome face.

"May I first purchase some dried meat and some bread to provision our travel bags?"

"Yes, how much would you care for?" she asked, opening the curing box behind her.

"Perhaps a pound would suffice." William watched the woman as she sliced the salted ham over the stone counter. He then asked, "Have you by any chance seen a gentleman with a lady passing through town this day?"

"Yes, we did have two travelers come through. They did not stay long. I noticed the carriage left a short while after arriving, which was rather strange."

"Did you see the lady come out of the inn later on perchance?"

"No, my dear sir. But that don't mean nothing. She could have gone all on her own through the alley behind the public house."

"Thank you for everything, ma'am," William said, as he paid for his purchases.

He then walked out of the store, looking around before locating Frank. He did not know which direction to take.

Frank had finished speaking with the livery stable boy while noticing William up the road. "William!" he called out.

"Yes, Frank. Have you found out anything?"

"The stable boy observed a lady with a man leave only a half-an-hour ago. We must hurry for we will be wasting precious time if we linger around here."

Thus renewed in their hopes, they proceeded towards the docks. The lad at the stable had heard the man mention the docks as he was passing by the livery door.

"This is good, Frank. But why the docks?" William queried, not wanting to entertain the thought as to why Katherin may be headed for the Southampton Port. They both rode their horses as hard as they could for fear of missing their quarry – before Katherin embarked a ship for parts unknown – perhaps.

They arrived at their destination in good time. There, they found many ships and boats docked at the loading piers.

Chapter 17

The day had been long and exhausting for Mr. Hampton. He arrived at the family home in such a state of unrest that the servants had not seen him so distressed since Madame Constance's death.

Miss Louise was beside herself. She made great efforts to calm Mr. Hampton from his ill-tempered attitude. She wished for him to be happy as he once was. However, Miss Louise had her own concerns related to Miss Katherin.

"Mr. Hampton! Are you quite certain the count has not been entirely honourable toward Miss Katherin?"

"No, I am not certain, for our discussion did not last long. Conversely, I did not feel satisfied with the answers the count provided."

"Would you allow me to speak with the count under the pretext of visiting Miss Katherin that is?" Miss Louise asked, simply intending to reassure Mr. Hampton.

"I'm not certain that such a visit would serve any purpose at this point, Miss Louise. I fear his lordship was suspicious of my last visit. I unfortunately was not as subtle as I wished to be, for my temper surfaced while speaking with the insufferable man," Mr. Hampton admitted shamefully.

"Allow me to make an attempt. I could visit under the pretence of spending time with Miss Katherin. His lordship should not be suspicious, for I will make efforts to assure him that I would be aiding with Katherin's education in the womanly arts and manners. This should reassure the count while I question Miss Katherin as to any indiscretion on his part. Do you not agree?" Miss Louise tried to be as practical as possible in her plan.

Mr. Hampton had to agree, for she made a lot of sense. He had not realized how astute the woman truly was, although he had engaged her for her intelligence and teaching abilities. She would be thus able to take over Mr. Brody's assignments in his absence such as presently. His personal affairs had not been resolved as he had hoped and was still absent from his post.

Perhaps, Mr. Hampton thought, that he should pay more attention to the activities of the persons in his service. "Have you ever considered a profession in the domain of jurisprudence, Miss Louise?" he asked, for it was becoming quite evident that he may not be the one in charge in his own house. He smiled while he was inquiring of her intention, despite his growing apprehension. And he truly wondered what other information he had not realized before this day. Perhaps he would have been reassured of Katherin's safety had he paid closer attention to other details. Grief can be a distractible aspect that affects the mind.

"I will be taking the children out for a special day tomorrow. I have been neglectful and would love to spend more time with them before they too are leaving the family home."

Miss Louise smiled with the delightful offer. She left to seek the children with the good news. She had spoken with the children not so long ago, asking for their full cooperation with their studies while their father was concerned with other matters. Once they knew their father was going to take them to town the next day, they bounced up and down with joy.

"Children! Please, you must finish your studies first. I beg of you; do not get ahead of yourselves!" she called out to them.

"Yes! Yes, we will!" came the loud shouts from the three of them.

"For the moment, however, you must remain seated." Miss Louise then managed to silence them.

They settled in for the remainder of the day while they concentrated on their studies, although their minds every so often would wander off with thoughts of the day's journey with their father.

Mr. Hampton went out to arrange for their excursion the following day. While organizing the hiring of the carriage, at the same time, he ordered another coach for Miss Louise's trip to visit Katherin. Once he felt all was set, he traveled into town. He wished to visit a close friend of his who may have information regarding the Count of Sussex. Mr. Hampton arrived at Mr. Monte Hastings's residence a short while later. He was invited into the brightly decorated drawing room where Monte was comfortably ensconced in a chair, smoking a cigar and reading the news sheet of the day.

"Edward! How nice of you to come!"

"Yes, I have been meaning to visit…."

"Ah, that is quite understandable in view of all the circumstances. What brings you out?"

"I thought perhaps we could have a conversation regarding some things that have been of some concern to me."

"Yes, yes, of course. Please do sit down." Monte gestured to the sofa. "It was good to see you at the debutantes' ball. I would hope that life is treating you well since your daughter's recent marriage to the Count of Sussex," Monte said, puffing on his cigar

134

and sipping on a glass of port he had poured himself not long before Edward had arrived.

"In fact I am here for that very reason," Edward said. "I am concerned. My daughter's marriage with the count has been of concern to me. Pray tell, how much do you know regarding the Count of Sussex?"

"First let me offer you something to drink." Monte rose and went to the liquor cabinet located behind his chair. He opened it, poured a glass for his guest and returned to his seat, offering the drink to Edward.

"Well let me see," Monte then said, "I have yet to learn of any new information, although I have heard that he had been looking for a bride for some time."

"Yes, I was also aware of this. Yet, there are some matters that do not seem quite plausible regarding his comportment. I had the opportunity to visit with his lordship yesterday. I had come across some disturbing accounts earlier that day. I will not say what this information contained, for the very nature of it may not be accurate or reliable, although it should be investigated at a later time. I've come to ask whether you have any knowledge that the count may have acted with conduct unbecoming to a gentleman in the past."

"I have not heard of this, although my good friend Ellis Linton will be arriving shortly. Perhaps we may ask whether he has heard of any indiscretion with regards to his lordship's actions," Monte said.

Edward Hampton frowned. "Ellis. Is he the renowned Ellis Linton of Lincolnshire?"

"Yes, the very same."

"His reputation does precede him indeed. And if he has any information regarding the Count of Sussex's comportment toward ladies of his acquaintance, it would be very helpful, I'm sure," Edward agreed.

"Ah! I do believe I hear approaching horses as we speak."

They both sat quietly while waiting for Ellis Linton of Lincolnshire to be shown into the drawing room. Not long afterward, the butler entered the room and bowed.

"Sir, Monsieur Ellis Linton is here to see you," he announced.

"Thank you, George."

"Ah, Ellis, how are you?" Monte asked, standing up to shake his friend's hand.

"I have been splendidly well, my dear Monte. Very fit indeed." Ellis smiled, instantly turning to Edward.

"This is Monsieur Edward Hampton, Ellis. Perhaps you two are already acquainted, are you not?"

Edward Hampton rose and bowed to Ellis Linton. "It is good to meet you, sir, although I have heard some excellent reports in advance of making your acquaintance today."

"Likewise, sir," Ellis said before sitting down in the chair facing the two companions.

"Let me pour you a drink," Monte offered, going to the liquor cabinet. "Would you prefer port or perhaps a cognac would be more to your taste?"

"A cognac, by all means, my dear Monte. I know you have the best in your cellar. Thus, if you don't mind, a drop of such nectar would be delectable indeed. Thank you."

As soon as the cognac was poured, Monte turned to his friend. "There you are, Ellis." He handed the snifter to him and sat down. "Edward here tells me that he has some concerns regarding the Count of Sussex, who, as you are aware, recently married his daughter. Have you heard of any pertinent information regarding his lordship's comportment toward ladies of his acquaintance?" Monte asked.

"I have heard that the man can be quite charming when he obtains what he seeks. Not many dare cross his path, or deny him his pleasure. He will not tolerate anyone to bar his passage or deny him anything," Ellis said, sipping on his drink after swirling the golden liquid around the snifter concertedly.

"I have heard reports that he has not always been what you may call a gentleman," Edward said. "Do you believe this to be the case, in the instance of my daughter?"

Chapter 18

The count made great efforts to arrive on time, yet he simply could not reach his destination in due course. He encountered unexpected and quite a few delays as he rode down the dirt path. He was headed to the docks to finalize his preparation for his travels abroad. A journey would give the impression of a gentle nobleman desirous to seduce his new bride. His goal was for his bride to view him as the knight in shining armour, so to speak – the man who rescued her from the clutches of vagrants and highway robbers. In the end the damsel would fall in love with him, of course. Katherin was young and likely desirous of a romantic attachment. All he had to do was to persuade her of his good and honourable intentions.

With this in mind, he plotted to have Katherin taken to a ship, and once there, he would rescue her, concluding his good deed, thus ensuring all would be well with his recalcitrant young bride.

At present however, the count was faced with yet another setback. As he sat waiting to pass, his lordship shouted, "Yes, my good man, you are definitely in the wrong with your animals crossing the road. How long will this take to clear these beasts from this path?" he called out with annoyance.

"Pardon me, my good sir, I cannot hear you with the noise of the sheep."

"Yes, yes, of course, yet another reason for you not to hurry." his lordship sounded quite annoyed.

"Sir, I cannot hear you?"

The count resorted to shouting and waving his arms about for the sheepherder to figure out what was being said.

"I beg your pardon, sir, I am moving them as quickly as I humanly can," he shouted back in his turn.

"At last, the insufferable man understands!" The count sat back, waiting for the clearing of the road with as much patience as he could muster.

Meanwhile, the following day, Mr. Hampton left for town with the children as was originally planned, whereby the governess set out to visit the count's home.

Miss Louise had not been on a road trip for quite some time. She had forgotten how lovely the green landscapes could be, while enjoying the fresh air. She could not understand why she had not gone on more outings of this sort. The trees displayed their splendid spring colours with flowers budding out, which produced the most spectacular beauty. However, an artist's paintbrush could not do equal justice to nature's own paintbrush. *The natural world can produce the most excellent colours*, she thought. At times, she wondered whether remaining a spinster and looking after someone else's children had been her best decision since it would have been quite delightful to exchange her thoughts with someone who could appreciate the natural splendour she was privileged to admire at this very moment.

The trip did not last very long however. She was approaching the count's mansion, where she would soon be applying her talents in the art of persuasion. The carriage pulled up to the front gate. The driver stopped before jumping down to open its door.

Cruel Providence

Shortly thereafter, he assisted the governess down the steps of the coach.

Miss Louise then said, "Do not set off too far, nor get too comfortable with resting for I know not when I will need to take my leave."

"Yes, ma'am," he reluctantly replied.

Miss Louise then walked up the three steps to the immense doors, and rapped against it with the large gold knocker.

Soon the door was opened. "Yes," the major d'homme answered, looking rather annoyed.

"Yes, I've come to visit Countess Katherin. May I come in?" She was not going to take no for an answer. She stepped inside the foyer directly – not waiting for the man's answer.

"I am afraid the countess is away at present, ma'am," the approaching butler said, bowing to her respectfully.

"Oh dear!" Miss Louise said, turning to him. "I had not received word of her departure. When did she leave?"

"It was very early yesterday morn, ma'am."

"I see. Would the count be with her then?"

"Yes, ma'am," the butler became impatient with this line of inquiry.

"Could I bother you for tea before my departure? It has been a long journey?" Miss Louise asked.

"As you wish. I will bring tea. Where would you like to have it?" he asked.

"Could I be so bold as to have it in the kitchen?"

"Yes, ma'am. I will arrange for tea. Please come this way." The butler led the way to the kitchen with Miss Louise not far behind him.

"I do appreciate your kindness for it has been such a long trip and I am quite parched," she added.

The butler kept walking towards the dining area with not so much as a word afterwards.

"Thank you," she said once she was shown to the table. The butler arranged for Miss Louise's tea and disappeared somewhere else into the house moments afterward.

The servants came through the kitchen to help out, and seemed pleased to have someone new with whom to converse, and a person who, by all appearances, was impeccably dressed.

"Is your tea as you like it, ma'am?"

"Oh yes, thank you," Miss Louise replied. This was her chance to speak with the other servants. "May I ask a few questions then?"

"Why yes, ma'am," the cook's aid answered eagerly. She had been taught not to be rude no matter the circumstances. And the present situation together with the person sitting at the kitchen table presented no threat to her demeanour. The guest was rather dressed in a fashionable manner.

"The count and countess departed suddenly, or was this a planned journey?"

"Yes, ma'am, it was sudden that is. His lordship mentioned it only on the eve of their departure, ma'am."

"Would you happen to know where their journey would take them?"

"Not exactly, though we did overhear something regarding the boats, ma'am."

"Did Countess Katherin seem happy then?"

"Not too sure, ma'am. She was nervous like, and did not say much to us."

"I see. Thank you for tea," Miss Louise said, rising to take her leave.

Cruel Providence

The maid escorted her out to the front door thanking her for her visit.

"You have been most delightful. One more question before I leave. Do you know when they would be returning?"

"Sorry, ma'am, no mention of that was ever made to any of us."

"Why thank you, you've been most gracious." They both curtsied to one another while the butler opened the door for Miss Louise. She stepped into the carriage before the driver closed the door on her and climbed aboard. He quickly snapped his whip to carry on their journey back to the Hampton's residence.

Meanwhile, Mr. Hampton was spending a fine day in town with the children. They had gone to the theatre where an afternoon puppet show was performing. They sat excitedly waiting for the play to begin while giggling with amusement. He heard them laughing; a sound he not heard for rather a long time. The sadness of losing his wife nearly killed him from a broken heart. Nevertheless, the children lost their mother too. They missed her dreadfully while their father withdrew from the world. It must have seemed as if they had no parental love, affection or even guidance. In turn, Mr. Hampton came to the conclusion that he must involve himself with their lives from this day forth. He turned to them. Young Edward was on one side of him, and the two girls, Jane and Genevieve sat on the other side. He extended his arms and gathered them in one gigantic embrace. The children were delighted with his show of affection. They all felt the love emanate from their father. They smiled from ear to ear.

Later that evening, the governess returned to the Hampton's residence where the carriage pulled up to the front door. She stepped out to enter the building, although she felt somewhat disappointed for not completing her task. The butler informed her that Mr. Hampton and the children were still away in town. She had hoped he would have a great afternoon with the children for it had been such a long time since they had some amusement in their precious little lives. There had been too much sorrow in this household, that they surely deserved an outing of this sort. Miss Louise was certain to approach Mr. Hampton regarding the outings recurring more often in the future. She was encouraged by his newfound reengagement in the children's lives.

Chapter 19

After an arduous ride, both men dismounted their horses. The air was thick with fog, but without delay, they set off in search of Katherin. After arriving at the docks, they inquired with the first sailor they came upon.

"Sir, would you happen to have seen a beautiful young lady with an older gentleman boarding this ship?" William asked, nodding in the direction of the vessel alongside the pier.

"Sorry, mate," the man replied. "There are plenty of young women boarding ships these days."

"Yes, I'm quite aware of the fact. However, this lady is a particularly beautiful woman with golden hair and the most extraordinary blue eyes I've ever come across," William said. "There is no doubt who ever lays eyes upon her will surely remember such a handsome young woman." It was clear that the man had been smitten.

"Not sure. Perhaps you should check with the captain on board. He'd be sure to watch every passenger boarding his vessel."

"Yes, lad," William replied. "Would you know who the captain of this ship is?"

"That'd be Captain Shore, my good sir," the sailor said with a trace of reproach in his voice, as if anyone important should have known.

"Thank you. Much appreciated." William bowed prior to boarding the ship with Frank not far on his heels. At last, William had a name to go on the ship so as to not look like a stowaway.

"Perhaps we'd be in luck," Frank said while climbing the gangway to board the *Discovery*.

"Yes, Captain Shore?" William bowed while speaking with whom he hoped was the captain.

"Yes, sir! Who's asking?" the captain demanded.

"William Hampshire, sir!"

"What can I do for you, Mr. Hampshire?"

"I was wondering whether you've seen a young woman boarding with an older gentleman. The older gentleman is the Count of Sussex," William said with notable desperation in his voice. He was well aware that both might have sailed already.

"Yes, sir. I did see a young woman come aboard. She'd be with an older gentleman, as you say. They boarded not ten minutes ago," the captain replied.

"May I have a word with them before you set sail, Captain?" William was coming to life at long last.

"Why I can't see the harm in that."

The captain instructed the second mate to comply with the gentleman's request to see his companions off. William and Frank followed the sailor to the berth where the couple was quartered. William was nervous. What would he say once he encountered his lordship and Miss Katherin?

"Here, sir, you will find the pair," the sailor told them, pointing to a well-appointed cabin afore deck.

"Thank you," Frank said, while the second mate turned to leave.

William rapped at the cabin's door. However, to their great disappointment, the gentleman who answered the door was not the count.

They had a few words then sadly they both left the ship.

Nevertheless they were determined to locate Katherin before the day was out.

Both men spent much of their time searching the docks for further clues as to Katherin's whereabouts.

Cruel Providence

They had not been too fortunate though, finding very little if any trace of her passage. Finally, Frank suggested that they return to the public house for some needed sustenance. They had not eaten, apart from a piece of ham and bread that William had bought in the village hours earlier. After being seated, they ate their bread with dried meat and cheese when a gentleman entered the public place.

"Aye, mate! Would you know where I could buy some thick ribbon and rope?" he enquired of the innkeeper.

William could only wonder why he'd be requesting these odd supplies. William and Frank finished eating and drinking in a hurry, and followed the man to the supply store down the street near the dock. They waited for the man to come out with his goods. When he re-appeared, they both followed him discreetly out to where he was headed.

"He boarded the *Fleetwood* ship. Should we board and follow him to his destination?" Frank suggested to William.

"Yes, why don't we?" William replied.

Both boarded the ship where some of the crew blocked their passage.

"Well, well looks who we've here?" the first mate questioned while rolling his 'r's.

"Pardon our intrusion, sir. We were wondering who the man was that came aboard not but a few moments before our arrival? Could you help us?" William braved the question with more and more sailors surrounding the two men.

"Hey yee hear him, mates? He wants to know who's aboard." He laughed.

"We do not mean to stir trouble." Frank tried to appease the brooding sailors.

"Looky here! We can sees you made loads of trouble as we caught you red handed!"

By now both men were wishing they had staked out the ship before traipsing up the gangway. Perhaps they could somehow talk their way out of this mess for the other option of fighting did not sit well with either of them.

"Now, we do understand how you feel. We did not know we were trespassing, but only seeking your assistance on the voyage. Where did you say you were sailing off again?" were William's efforts to remedy the situation by making enquiries as though they were to depart with the ship.

"We'd not say!"

"Why, I thought you did. Did he not, William?" Frank caught on by playing right along.

"Yes, yes, I do believe you did, good man. Was it to the new land, or did you mention France?" William asked.

"Nah! We didn't."

"Yes, we were wondering how much to board so we can travel along with you good lads," William queried.

"Let me see, so yee want to pay to travel with us common sailors?"

"Well of course, we were looking to contract out your services for we are in need to journey across the sea. What say you name your price, and we can see if you are given us the better price than the freighter over there. We wanted to talk with you gents before coming aboard," William prompted for a better reaction from the crowd.

"What's going down here?" came a bellowing shout from the other side of the gathering. The men dispersed rapidly, allowing for the captain to ascertain what was happening on his ship. "You two lads in some kind of trouble? You have taken me men out of commission?" He turned to the crew. "We be sailing in a few minutes, so best be getting to your post!" he ordered. The crew ran to their designated posts with such speed that only Frank and William remained standing beside him.

"Thank you, Captain. We were just leaving not wanting to detain you longer than necessary," Frank confessed to the captain.

"Well yee best be getting off for we sail as we speak. Now move; and that goes for all you slackers, pull anchor, we shove her off!" the captain yelled.

William and Frank made haste, running off the ship most hurriedly to avoid any more unpleasant scenes with the crew. To their relief, the ship sailed to where they hoped it would never return. It was unfortunate that they hadn't had the chance to discover what the man wanted with his rope.

"What do we do next?" Frank questioned, for at the moment, he felt they were travelling in circles.

"Not certain." William was resigned to the fact that finding Katherin was more arduous than one could have imagined, and they were clearly running out of time.

Chapter 20

Katherin had been repeatedly pushed, shoved, pulled with no hope of ever seeing her husband. She had frequently demanded to see him, but had never been given an answer as to his whereabouts. Ultimately, she had been brought to the docks. She knew there was something amiss because she had never been treated with such coarseness or detestable manner in her entire life. Could this be an error, or perhaps she was having a terrible nightmare and required to be awakened? Thus far, her only memory of her entourage was that of love and gentleness. This unfortunate occurrence was not something to which she had been accustomed.

Upon arriving at the waterfront, the air was filled with a thick misty fog. She could not see but a mere five feet in front of her. The air was chilly. Katherin could only wrap her woollen shawl tighter around her neck, as the cold seemed to penetrate her to the core. Her growing fear was that she would never feel warm again. By far, it was the worst day of her youthful life.

"Where are you taking me? I've not seen the count as promised," she complained yet again.

"If I were yee, Missy, I would stay quiet as a mouse," was her abductor's snickered reply put forth in a vile whisper.

His sinister appearance and nearness provoked shivers to course down Katherin's spine. They arrived at a ship where he escorted her towards the gangway to board it. Katherin could not see which vessel she was boarding, given that the fog prevented her from seeing very far on either side of her. Once they boarded, she was brought below deck. When Katherin entered the cabin, she was shoved onto a bed. The kidnapper turned and quickly closed the door behind him, locking it from the outside. Katherin was quick to reach for the door, yet before she could turn the handle, it was securely locked. She could hear an eerie laughter from her captor, producing chills to raise hair at the nape of her neck. This was not what she had imagined for herself. As a newlywed, she had heard that the first few months of marriage were a very blissful time. She returned to the bed and sat down, wondering what she should do next. Could the ruthless man be telling her the truth that the count would be meeting her? She had no idea for the coarseness of her captor's behaviour would suggest he would not be keeping his word. She would have imagined a more gentle conduct, as she could not believe the count to be so heartless as to treat her with such disregard.

Finally, she heard footsteps above her. Perchance the count had arrived? He would certainly rescue her from this damp and cold place. In spite of this, she did not hear footsteps descending to the lower deck, but simply more steps sounding above her head as if the crew had boarded the vessel presently. It must have been so as the ship started moving. What was happening? She had wrapped herself with the only thin blanket from the bed to keep the cold out while she pondered upon her fate.

"Hello! Can anyone hear me?" Katherin called out. No reply. Had the count not boarded, for surely he would have joined her soon thereafter. She had no knowledge as to what she should do. The world in which she had dwelled before today had not properly prepared her for such a misadventure. Perhaps she should have read more books to expand her knowledge of the world. It would have provided her with some awareness in case of such an unexpected turn of events. Katherin rose from the bed, making another attempt at prying the door open. Again she was unsuccessful as the door was unyielding without a key. She crouched down to the floor in order to view under the door, peeking outside of her small cabin. Her only view was the bottom step at the end of the corridor. No one was in sight. The fact explained why there were no responses to her cries.

Meanwhile, the ship had sailed for some unknown destination. Not one sailor had come down to the lower deck for what felt like hours. She sat on the floor by the door, and began to feel seasick. Her stomach felt terribly upset. As she tried to lie on the bed, the queasiness would not leave her. She finally lost the battle, however harsh this was for her, and emptied the contents of her stomach into the tiny chamber pot.

Feeling somewhat better, she lay still on the bed. Katherin felt hours passing while the ship moaned and creaked as it made its way to a distant shore. The time afforded her with reflection of her father, siblings, and how the growing distance with each wave drew them farther apart. Sleep at last overtook her to dream of a better adventure.

The ship sailed on for quite some time when the weather began to turn for the worst. Katherin awoke frightened. The sound of rushing waves hitting the sides of the ship was simply terrifying. She had dreamt of being captive where the sailors had attacked her. Her heart raced with expectation of it exploding at any moment. She found herself soaked with perspiration while chilled to the core. She wrapped the cover around her and clutched it to her chin to avoid freezing to death. The darkness did not help. With the weather turning foul, she could not see outside to estimate the time of day. The ship rocked back and forth whereby she was faced with another bout of sea-sickness. She vomited again in the small container beside her bed. The smell of it could have made her even sicker than she already was.

At last she heard someone unlocking the door. She immediately pulled the covers tightly to her neck for fear had gripped her with the memory of her latest dream. Her heart beat so rapidly that the sound would have been deafening to anyone close to her. The door opened wide with the same brute who abducted her walking in before kicking it shut with his foot.

"Now looky yee, all wrapped up like a mummy," he announced, grinning. "I wonder if yee missed me." He chuckled with such an evil hilarity, that it sent chills down Katherin's back.

"Where are we?" Katherin asked after finally finding her voice.

"Don't yee worry? We're on our way to a New World yee see," he replied still snickering.

"I do not understand. You alleged we would be meeting the count. Where is he?" Katherin queried timidly.

"Let's says we has a change of plans."

"What do you mean?" Katherin sounded more frightened than she would have liked to admit.

"I says: don't worry!" he repeated, how ever forceful this statement came out of his filthy mouth.

Katherin felt as though she was treading dangerous waters. She did not want to anger this wicked man for fear of being unable to escape him while on board this vessel. She despised her abductor. This feeling of intense anger was totally unknown to her.

The man came ever so close to Katherin's face, that she could smell liquor on his breath. Although she had never felt as scared as she was feeling presently, and not knowing whether screaming would prove to be wise, she decided not to shout for assistance.

He came closer and lifted her head toward his face. He held a bottle of rum he had drank empty after entering the room. Through his parted lips, Katherin could see his crooked and decaying teeth. Along with greasy matted hair, the face of him made for a scene that only nightmares could conjure up. He was portly and short in stature with non-descript features and a heavy gait. He was not a gentle man, certainly not the sort of gentleman to which Katherin had been accustomed. He brought his lips over hers. She pulled back with all her might, pushing him away with her legs. In his drunken state, she had an easy time to knock him down to the floor. She dropped the blanket and rushed over to the door, but found it locked. By this time, the drunken man had recovered and was now lunging at her, pulling her to the floor with him. Katherin let out a scream, not only from fright, but also from falling so abruptly. Yet, in her enraged state she recovered so quickly that, with such speed, she managed to escape his grasp. She ran to the bed, grabbed her blanket and wrapped the felon in it as tightly as she could. She had done so with such rapidity that she surprised herself for she knew not from where her strength came. It was as if she had been assisted, or guided by some force that she could not explain. Perhaps it was instinctive. But from where did this unforeseen assistance come?

Cruel Providence

The man rolled down with a sigh of drunkenness in his tightly wrapped woollen blanket. With no way out of this sausage wrap, he finally lay still.

Katherin looked around the room and upon finding the bottle, she knocked him out. She did not know what she was to do afterward, although she felt the immediate threat from her kidnapper had been averted.

She sat down on her bed, speculating as to her next move. She felt no matter what she would do, it would not return her home safely for the fact was obvious: trying to escape a vessel while at sea was futile. What could she do?

Chapter 21

Upon the count's return to the inn, he discovered that his plan was already in motion. It would not be long before Katherin would be in his arms, vastly affectionate for his good deed of rescuing her by the one and only knight. He paid the innkeeper for all their services before proceeding to the docks as planned. He would finally be able to put the remainder of his devious plan into action.

It hadn't taken long for Count Leanard to reach the docks. He stepped out of the carriage to find the fog excessively thick and seeing the vessel he sought was challenging, if not impossible.

"Good day! Could you be so kind as to direct me to the Anna Fitz?" the count questioned the sailor passing by.

"No, sir, I'd be taking another ship!" he replied as he continued walking past the count in his haste to board his own vessel.

The count kept on with his search, without any success. He decided to walk to the mercantile store for the owner would surely know where the Anna Fitz was docked. The owner was preparing to close for the night, as he entered the store.

"And what can we get you, my good sir?" the store attendant asked, motioning to his lordship to step in, out of the cold.

"I would like to know if you would kindly direct me to the Anna Fitz?"

"Well, sir, she had docked earlier, over by the eastside of the harbour."

"Thank you, sir," the count replied, hurrying out the door.

Cruel Providence

As soon as he found it, he rushed up the gangway whereupon *she* immediately let the mooring cordage go and pulled away from the pier. The Anna Fitz was sailing for the count's rendezvous with his captive bride. Count Leanard had been very anxious to set sail, for the next phase of his truly innovative plan was about to begin. His lordship affixed a most wicked grin on his lips, while he thought of his ingenious plot. No one would ever suspect him capable of spinning such a web of deceit. Surely Mr. Hampton would be very grateful for rescuing his little angel, and would be forever in his debt. Perhaps he could be so wise as to help others with such a deed? He laughed to himself. The count then went to see the captain to ensure their entire voyage would be timed precisely, thus ensuring that he would not miss intercepting the ship on which Katherin had set sail.

In the meantime, William Hampshire and his friend Frank Shelby were resting at the inn where they had arranged to stay the night. While William sat thinking of the situation, he couldn't help but feel that every hour that passed was in effect an added difficulty when it came to annul the marriage between Count Leanard and Miss Katherin Hampton. He had no idea whether the marriage had been consummated. At this point, should he cease his pursuit, he knew in his heart that he would not rest until he had done everything to insure her happiness, whether it be with him, or with her new husband. It was then that both men overheard the count speaking with the innkeeper in the hallway. They decided it would be worthwhile to follow the count to his rendezvous, which location they clearly heard from the count's own lips. What kind of a man would put his new wife in such a precarious situation, William could not imagine.

"You heard the count, Frank! We must do something to help Katherin," William uttered with renewed concern for Katherin's welfare.

"I do believe she is Countess Katherin presently. We may not be in a position to do much to rescue her," Frank noted, knowing full well that the task at hand would be very risky, not to say dangerous, should they manage to foil the count's plot.

The conversation they overheard had clearly indicated to both men that the count could not be trusted. This fact presented a serious threat.

"Frank, we must try to do what we can! Do you not agree?"

"I would gladly assist, should you require my services for you know where my loyalty lies," Frank stated.

"Yes, I do understand. Should there be any other way around this disastrous turn of events, I would gladly revise our intent. However, I do not know what else we could do. You are a good friend, and I am especially grateful for all that you have done thus far."

"Yes, of course. You do have a point regarding Countess Katherin's predicament. So, what do you propose we do now?"

"We have to follow Katherin to her destination, where ever that may be. Of course, there is no indication as to the direction in which her vessel set sail. It could be any of the compass points."

"Then it would serve Katherin best if we were to waste no time in locating her or her vessel before worst fate befalls her."

Cruel Providence

Both men went about questioning anyone with information which would assist them in locating the count for it would certainly lead them to Katherin. For a second time, they arrived at the docks to see the storekeeper leaving his mercantile establishment.

"Sir," William drew the man's attention. "We were wondering whether you might assist us."

"What may I do for you this time round then?"

"You could tell us if you have seen Count Leanard pass through here or perchance stop in your shop?" William asked, knowing that most men would come for last minute supplies before they set sail.

The storekeeper had not known the count to see him, but for a small fee, he was willing to talk.

William was exasperated with the storekeeper; however he felt he had no other choice, except for offering the coins the man demanded for loosening his tongue.

"I will pay you once I receive valuable information. Could you speak the truth on what you know?"

The mercantile man did not see any point in pressing his luck. The gentleman before him was not to be divested of his coins easily it appeared. Thus, he gladly recounted what he heard. An older man in company of a young woman bought supplies before their journey earlier in the evening. He also recalled a smartly dressed gentleman, who had come in to enquire about his ship. "The fog been as thick as it was, the gentleman could not locate it."

"Would you know where the gentleman and the young woman were headed?"

"The two who came in said something about the New World," the storekeeper replied.

"I understand. Would you know of any vessel headed in that direction tonight, sir?" William demanded, knowing he had little time to waste.

"Why yes, the *Mayfair* will be leaving this night. Should you hurry you may have time to reach it before it sails."

"Thank you. You've been most helpful and for your great service, here is payment." William offered the man several more coins.

William and Frank then ran to the Mayfair anxious to reach it before departure.

"I must leave word before departing," Frank said, as they strode toward the handsome vessel. "I fear it will not be a short voyage, and father would be most distressed should he not receive word, William."

"Yes, I do believe you have a point. We will summon someone to deliver a message," William agreed. He had not thought this through. His distraught behaviour, in the past few days, was all but consuming his mind.

They left word before boarding the *Mayfair*, paying their fare before embarking upon the ship.

The vessel departed shortly thereafter, in the direction of the New World that would hopefully bring William closer to his beloved Katherin. William felt obliged to put an end to the count's evil plan and be assured that Katherin was not in imminent danger.

Chapter 22

Mr. Hampton was beside himself with worry for his little kitten. How could he have been so short-sighted as not to see how the past few weeks did not provide Katherin the security he had vowed for her to his dying wife? Had he known the count's intentions of taking Katherin away so quickly after their wedding and without warning, he would have certainly made other arrangements for her. However one thing was clear, the count did not have his daughter's best interest at heart. Therefore, Mr. Hampton would not have allowed the marriage to take place so early in the courtship. In his pursuit of justice, he had sent out messengers to locate his daughter – to no avail. There was not as much as a trace of her. Where could the count have gone? He had since sent out, not one but two messengers. This time he was quite hopeful to receive word at any moment. Meanwhile, he had not been able to work, nor sleep since speaking with the governess after her visit with the servants at the count's home. He could only sit and wait for word of his lovely daughter.

One of the messengers sent out to locate Miss Katherin questioned a number of innkeepers and dock workers to obtain snippets of information regarding the young lady's whereabouts. However easy this assignment seemed, he could not find much in the way of details. The only information he was able to gain was that a young lady with the same description had boarded a freighter ship, which did not seem plausible. The messenger was truly puzzled at this point. Miss Katherin, a countess by then, would certainly be more likely to board a passenger ship than a freighter. Yet, there was no information on any countess boarding such a vessel. The messenger spent the remainder of the day seeking answers, receiving no tangible information as to the young woman's whereabouts. Then again, he did hear of a count who boarded a ship headed for France. With information in hand, the messenger rode back to Mr. Hampton's residence to report his findings as quickly as he could ride.

Moreover, the messenger had received word of a sighting at the Westward Inn near the Southampton docks. When news of the count's departure reached Mr. Hampton, he made arrangements to depart for parts unknown – probably Europe, leaving the governess in charge.

Katherin's father rode part of the night, arriving at the docks quite early, where he, too, would board a ship headed for France, but not before paying a visit to the innkeeper at the Westward Inn. The carriage pulled up in front of the inn where Mr. Hampton gave the driver a purse of coins for his diligent ride through the countryside.

"Please be so kind as to wait outside for I shall not be long," he told the coach driver. Mr. Hampton then went inside the inn to gather more information regarding his daughter's disappearance.

He approached the innkeeper, asking, "Pardon me, my good sir, I would like to know if you would be so kind as to recall the presence of a young woman in your establishment, yesterday."

"I might have, sir. What would that information get me?" The innkeeper recognized a man with coins in his waistcoat when he saw one; and this man had pockets full of them, he reckoned.

Cruel Providence

"I am sure to pay you handsomely, my good man, for any information you may have."

"I'll be sure to tell you all I know upon you putting a coin or two in that palm of mine." The man extended an open hand across the counter, into which Mr. Hampton dropped a couple of coins as requested. "Would you have heard or seen her?" he then demanded, his tone leaving no doubt in the innkeeper's mind that he should not ask for any more than he truly deserved.

"She is a young girl about five feet two inches tall with blond hair, elegantly dressed," Mr. Hampton went on.

"Why I do believe we had such a young lady here not long ago. She arrived with…" As the innkeeper hesitated to continue, Mr. Hampton put another coin on the counter but kept his hand over it. "Perhaps this can aid your memory?"

The Innkeeper licked his lips before saying, "I do believe it was the Count of Sussex who accompanied her."

"How long since they departed?" Mr. Hampton queried.

"Well, her ladyship left before the count returned, which I thought quite odd."

"Do you mean to say the count left her here alone without chaperone?" Mr. Hampton was clearly outraged.

"Yes, he had to leave for a short time."

"Do you have any idea where the young woman has disappeared?"

"No, sir, but I believe the count was headed for France."

"Thank you for your troubles," Mr. Hampton said before leaving the inn.

He then made the necessary arrangements to approach the count in France for such a cad would not dupe him again. He was spoiling for a fight and with his growing anger; Edward would not rest easy until he faced the blighter himself. He hastily sent a message to his governess regarding his departure time, and not knowing his return trip, he left that area of the note blank.

Mr. Hampton left the English shores only hours prior to arriving in France, upon which he had never set foot. He was not certain how he would proceed to find the count on foreign soil. Truth be told, he did not know what awaited him there either.

Miss Louise was also quite surprised of Mr. Hampton's sudden departure to France. He was not a man who took to adventurous travels effortlessly. You could say he had become most tiresome, almost a recluse, especially after the untimely death of his late wife. He was not one to partake in uncertain business ventures easily either, for in the business world his reputation was considered rather sound. It was probably the untimely death of Constance that brought out the risk in him. Of late, he had let down his guard, for he not only would suffer emotionally but, she feared, financially.

To the count's great disappointment, he discovered that his ship would not meet with Katherin's rescue as originally planned. His lordship was extremely angered for he was most anxious to consummate his marriage with the exquisite Katherin of Sussex. What was he to do now that her whereabouts were unknown? The count arrived in France and began seeking word of his new bride. To his great displeasure, no news came forth. No one had seen the young countess. He decided to wait the night in hopes that her ship would be docking the following day.

The following day the count was terribly impatient and foul-tempered. He had not anticipated his wife to be taken away from him. He knew he had been duped once the freighter did not materialize as planned. No such vessel was due to reach the coast of France in the near future. He could only stew in anger. Should he ever encounter Mr. Cathers once more, he would kill the man for such a betrayal as no one had ever dared deceiving him or would even attempt to do so.

Before the count could define a new plan in pursuit of his lovely bride, he was confronted with another problem of quite a different nature. Mr. Hampton had arrived from England and, upon coming face to face with him, had challenged him to a duel.

The count felt confident of winning such a ridiculous confrontation, however, he had reservations in the matter of a duel. He knew he could kill the old man, but he also knew that this was not the virtuous quality he wanted to display in the countess's eyes, and in effect this would not win her affections. Katherin would never forgive him for such an act against her father. Should he agree to the challenge put forth by Mr. Hampton, the count would have to keep it from reaching his bride's ears.

During the early part of the morning, the count made great efforts to stop the silly duel; however, Mr. Hampton was not to be civil in any ways or manners. Nor was Mr. Hampton being reasonable about allowing a truce, but rather he had accused the count of deception. This had never occurred before either, and he would duel to restore his honour according to the 14th century edict. Could there be any recourse?

Perhaps the action of killing her father in a fair duel would be the easiest endeavour he would undertake ever since he thought of leaving his house with Katherin two days ago now. However, the combat was set for noon the following day, and the count was somewhat nervous for it had been a long time since he last held an epee in his hand.

Mr. Hampton had been extremely angry when he learned that his daughter had been left unaccompanied and unattended at the Westward Inn. He had been so enraged in fact that his demeanour had reached the limit of all reason. He wished he could have been calmer, for his ire had resulted in him calling a duel with the count. It had been a very long time since he had practiced. He had been quite the fencing master in his younger days, but presently, he had to admit that with his depression and lack of exercise, his skills had suffered.

He was able to practice with a duelling partner for the following morning however. After practicing for only a short while, he found his breathing had been laboured. He decided to rest for an hour before the duel. After which he felt much better. He wondered whether he should have reasoned this situation before challenging the count, a much younger man, into a duel of honour. Perhaps, he would be killed. Then what would become of the children?

He finally made a choice not to think of death for he surely would not be able to proceed with the duel. Should he run, he would have to forfeit the entire matter. He would be looked upon as a coward. Surely the failure to face the challenge would be viewed as weakness on his part. What's more, turning his back on this duel now would not bode well in the business world. Therefore, he felt compelled to follow through with his initial decision whether it proved to be his last.

Chapter 23

Katherin had sat for hours with no real solution in sight when a moan came from the drunken brute lying on the floor. She had ensured her captive would not attack her. He was wrapped tightly with the cover, which she wished she could use against the cold that seemed to have permeated the cabin in the last few hours. She truly wondered whether she might be taking a trip past hell itself. She was currently faced with yet another dilemma. She wondered what to do with her abductor. She outwitted him and he was now her prisoner. However, at present, he was stirring and would soon be causing her more grief.

"What's this I ask?" he suddenly bellowed.

Fear gripped Katherin's entire body. She had never felt so frightened of another human being before today. She swallowed and faced him as he tried unravelling the blanket from around him.

Still staring at the wiggling, idiotic figure, but calmer now, Katherin said, "Sir, you would be best to keep silent for I should be tempted to silence you once again." She had no idea from where this new courage came.

"You would not?" he hissed at her.

"I am certain you know that I am quite capable of silencing you, do you not, sir!"

"Yee may sound all mighty, but should yee be in the opposite position, yee'd be grovelling with pleas of death to end your miserable existence," he uttered as he tried in vain to free himself from his wrap.

"At the moment, I am reminded that it is you who is the captive. You may be wise to remind yourself of this."

"Yeah! This comes forth from yee, lass," he spouted off laughing as though she had repeated a laughable riddle.

"Again, I repeat. You should remain silent," she loudly advised him.

"Or what?" he shouted back.

Katherin rose, crossed the floor to where the man lay. "I am very serious. Should you continue to shout at me, I will have no choice but to follow through with my threats," she went on, staring at him while holding the empty rum bottle over his head.

"I'm not afraid. Yee mistake yerself." He glared back at her, testing her bluff.

Katherin reached up high, grasping the bottle tightly, and quickly hit him on the head, rendering him unconscious. Katherin felt sick, for she had never acted in such a disturbing way before today. How could she have been so cruel, not once but twice in one day? She could not answer the question for she knew only fear was in control of her life at the moment. She also had no idea how she would continue the voyage if he should be in control once more. But should she free him of his bondage – only out of compassion – she would surely be killed. Katherin glanced around the cabin, searching for some rope to secure his hands. If she were able to bind his wrists at least she would finally be able to lay down her head to sleep. Besides, her stomach was clearly not at its best and in need of the rest. She managed to tie him around the pipe located in one of the corners of the cabin with torn pieces of her blanket. Once she completed the deed, she was confident that he would be out of harm's way.

"There!" she said out loud, feeling convinced that he was fairly well tied up. "Perhaps, I can rest now that you are secure," she whispered to him, as she did not want to wake him. Katherin took the blanket and wrapped herself in it before falling asleep rather quickly.

Katherin awoke hours later with her prisoner shouting at her.

"Let me out of here! Let me out, yee dirty little wench!"

"It is you again," she hollered in her turn. "Do you not know how to silence yourself? I would gladly assist you in that regard, but not wanting to cause brain injury by striking your skull once more."

"When I free meeself, and yee can be sure of it, yee will wish yee caused me brain damage," he retorted.

"Now, we have been over this once before, and please do not give me reasons to strike again. I would not hesitate either; you can be assured of that."

"What the devil!" he said, as he rethought his position. "At the very least bring food, yee wench?"

"You speak as though I have liberty to walk about this ship. I will not risk being someone's captive again."

"Then be so good as to try to find some grub before I starve meeself to death!"

"I do not know where to acquire this grub. I do not want to be placed in harm's way, should I make the effort."

"Listen to me. Yee need not be scared should yee relieve me hands of this rope, I would be only too happy and fetch us somethin' to eat." He tried being nice.

"I cannot! I am sure I would sorrowfully be disappointed with your conduct."

"I give yee me word, lass," he replied, raising his voice slightly.

"I cannot. Your word has no meaning!"

"Then I will trust yee to fetch grub by giving yee the way to where it is, lass. Now pay close attention. Yee must go up the stairs to the deck. Yee should turn left to find the food barrels. You'd not be seen at this hour. I promise it'd be the safest time."

"I will only attempt it once." Katherin gave into his constant pleas, as long as it provided the silence she desperately wanted. With that agreement, her prisoner reluctantly gave up the key to the door.

Katherin wrapped the cover around her shoulders before she unlocked and opened the door slightly to peer around for any traffic. Once assured that the coast was clear, she opened the door where she had her first glimpse of the outdoors. Up above were clear skies, with an endless sea of stars. They appeared brilliant against the darkened heavens. Katherin silently crept up to the deck, looking cautiously around her for any sailors. With the light of the full moon illuminating her path, she could see the barrels he spoke of not far from where she crouched down on the top step. She looked in both directions and once all was clear, she dashed toward them. She opened the first one. It reeked. She swiftly replaced the lid. She moved to the second barrel and found some dried flat bread that appeared somewhat edible. She took a few pieces of it before looking into the third, where she luckily found some dried meats, of which she grabbed a handful. She tucked them into her dress and then turned to disappear down below deck. At that moment, she spotted a sailor approaching, but she dodged behind the post where she hoped she would not be seen. The sailor walked past while Katherin's heart pounded a loud drumbeat in her chest. She glanced around prior to descending the stairs to safety. She entered the cabin to find the man had disappeared. She closed the door and raced up the stairs once more. One thing was certain; she was not about to let anyone capture her again. She hid among the lifeboats where it was unlikely she would be discovered. At the very least, she had food to keep her for a short while in the event the journey proved longer than anticipated.

Katherin had hid well for she had escaped the tyranny of her abductor for most of the journey. Sorrowfully, she had not resisted seeking water after several days at sea. She had not thought of how she would survive without water that seemed to be all around her. She had already escaped the peering eyes of her abductor by seeking water during the night, and returning safely to her haven. She remained hidden until she could no longer resist another venture as thirst had driven her out in the open, seeking the necessary nourishment to ensure her survival. On the final days of the journey, Katherin crept to the barrels, but as she opened the barrel, it was unfortunately empty. She had been terribly disappointed for she knew she could not hold up much longer without at the very least some water. She decided to run to where she knew water was kept, though she ran right into her kidnapper. "Oh God!" she blurted as he grabbed her arm in a vice-like grip.

The moon was not bright this evening and without it she was cornered. It was to her advantage not to be seen, however, the dim moon proved to be her undoing.

"Well, looky what's the cat dragged back up here?" He made fun of her misfortune.

"Let me go?" she demanded.

"Yee will not escape again. I do have plans for yee once we dock," he told her while watching her reactions, which were rewarding in themselves.

"My father would pay handsomely for my release, as long as I am not harmed that is," she told him as a matter-of-factly.

"I can fetch a great sum for yee. I have me connections. So I'd save yee breathe if I's be yee, little lass, and believe me I have a couple of strikes on your ladyship."

"I would think that if I was unharmed and without bruises, I would fetch a larger sum for you."

"That may be, but what do I gets out of it for me?"

"I will not escape; you have my word, sir." She made every effort to save her skin.

"Yee won't be escaping the hold I'd be tossing' yee into." He pushed her down the few stairs and she fell awkwardly. Once she landed, he swiftly opened a floor hatch leading to the hull of the ship, shoving her down into the hold.

Katherin felt pain in her knees, elbows and head. Her head was so bruised after she landed in her new home that the bump on her forehead swelled to an awful lump. She yelled out for help for a short while before she fell into a deep sleep that she only could hope would be her last painful experience.

The voyage continued for a couple more days.

They had finally docked with great relief to the sailors, as food rations had not lasted the full journey. They were all thankful to be on solid ground to seek out a decent meal and some ale. Most of all, the men wanted to find themselves with women along with the ale to celebrate their arrival.

Katherin had slipped in and out of consciousness for the remainder of the voyage. As she opened her eyes now, she could not focus, while her entire body felt as though she was in agonizing pain. She was doubled over with unbearable stomach spasms. Upon arrival, she was not in good condition and once her captor had seen her, he himself was displeased. He felt that he would have to prepare her, and should he get a great sum for her, he may very well retire from his wicked ways. Perhaps he could even settle down with a milkmaid. After opening the hatch, he grabbed her arm to raise her from the dead, as it appeared she remained rather lifeless. He carried her to the bed laying her down. He then felt an overwhelming desire to take her for himself. She appeared as an angel, so beautiful, and while she remained unmoving, she was not running away from him, nor was she mouthing off. He could keep her for himself, though once she regains consciousness; she would no doubt be spouting forth and making all his efforts to please her for naught. He shook off this ridiculous notion, and slapped her on the shoulder, then on her face to wake her.

"Wake, best wake!" he shouted while his hand came down hard on her cheek the second time. Katherin stirred slightly from the pain. Her entire body felt numb, if not aching and, in places, in awful pain.

"Wake!' he again shouted in attempts to bring her out from her unconscious state.

"Mm," she mumbled feebly.

"We's best leave this retched ship. Get up," he screamed in Katherin's ears.

Cruel Providence

Katherin still did not budge. He again felt slightly alarmed for the idea that she would not fetch him the desired purse would be a considerable disappointment. He grabbed her body and slung it over his shoulder, carrying her off the ship. He caught a carriage to a nearby inn where he could revive her, and somehow make her presentable and her appearance reasonably lifelike so as to fetch the wealth he desired. He arrived at the East Inn where he carried her inside. His arrival did not go unnoticed by the patrons.

"Can I help you, sir?" the innkeeper asked.

"I'd like a room for a few days," he stated.

"Do you require a doctor, sir?"

"No! She has passed out from too much drink," he offered by way of an explanation.

"Ah, very well," he agreed while smiling. He took a room key, handed it to the sailor.

Katherin was carried up a flight of stairs to the room before he set her down on the bed. She had not moved since leaving the ship. He possibly should have summoned a doctor, but not understanding the severity of the situation while she lay motionless, looking unwell and pale as snow, he did not do so. He had seen dead people that had more colour, however, and most likely, it would need a miracle in order to bring this fair maiden back to the living.

Chapter 24

On the Mayfair, the time proved very difficult for
William. He could not think of anything besides the
woman who had captivated his heart in such a way
that could only be described as an ardent love. He
was a bird in a cage for all to see how he mourned the
loss of his soul mate. He gazed out to sea as though
he were searching for Katherin over the endless swell,
within the clouds that decorated the horizon. He had a
forlorn look about him, which did not pass unnoticed
to his friend.

Frank stared at William. The latter was clearly
troubled. Frank had never seen William in such a
captivated state before meeting Katherin Hampton.
There had been plenty of women before, who had
gladly thrown themselves at William's feet for he was
indeed a very handsome man. It was not only
William's good looks, but also his charm and
sincerity that brought women to him with adoration,
for you could rarely find a more genuine man as
William. Frank wanted to assist his friend in his every
enterprise, although he simply did not know whether
this would bring him together with Katherin.
Conceivably, it was William's misfortune to fall in
love with the one woman who had already been
spoken for. According to Frank no good would ever
come out of this cat and mouse chase. At this point,
crossing an ocean to rescue a damsel in distress, with
whom William could scarcely hope to spend but a
few moments, seemed insane if truth be told. While
they stood overlooking the horizon of yet another day
gone by, watching waves rolling past their great ship,
Frank wondered whether they were too foolish to turn

back. But Frank was a true friend and would do whatever William required.

The evening had been ever so colourful where the scene highlighted a shimmering sunset, lighting not only the sky, but also the sea below. They had been on the ship for what felt reminiscent of weeks, without seeing the approaching coast. But through scrutinizing the horizon, Frank thought he could see a form appear in the remote distance.

"Finally, William! We are in sight of the Americas. Are you not pleased?" Frank questioned.

William did not raise his head towards the view of which Frank spoke. "William, are you ill?"

"I beg your pardon? Did you say something, Frank?" William finally answered.

"I simply mentioned our arrival to the New World, William."

"Yes, that is excellent!" William replied with a smile. His effort to show Frank that he was not totally ignoring him was scarce.

"Yes, what say we do after we land?" Frank questioned.

"We find her, and with good fortune, rescue her from a fate that I have no doubt will be her demise. I have a strong belief that she will not live long with such a man as the Count of Sussex," William admitted.

"Yes, you may be right. Do you know of anyone we could summon for aid, and perhaps request lodging?"

A few sailors walked past them discussing their imminent docking at the port of Boston.

"Yes, I do believe we have relations who crossed the sea several years past. I should like to see my distant uncle," William replied.

The ship was rapidly closing in on the horizon. It wasn't long before they entered the harbour and docked. Both men anxiously got off the ship signalling for a carriage that had pulled up the street to pick up new comers.

"Yes, sir. Where would you two gents be headed for?" the coachman asked.

"Should you perhaps know a man named Mr. Hampshire?" William questioned the driver while not knowing whether the question sounded unreasonable.

"Would this be the same man as Mr. Earl Hampshire, sir?" the driver enquired.

"Yes, the very same. Could you take us there?" William sounded rather excited to know they would most likely have a place to stay, and perhaps if all went well, his uncle may have news of Katherin's fate should she be lodged in the general vicinity of his residence.

The carriage pulled up to Earl Hampshire's home. William thanked the driver after paying for their fare. Both men entered the front courtyard and knocked at the door. A servant answered the door speaking briefly to the two men before proceeding to announce their arrival.

Uncle Earl was extremely pleased to welcome his nephew. "How are you, lad? I had no idea you would be sailing to our parts. Should there have been word of your voyage, I have not received it. Come in please." Earl invited them both into the parlour.

William made the introduction. "Uncle Earl, may I present Frank Shelby. He is a very dear friend of mine." He turned to Frank. "Frank, this is my uncle; Earl Hampshire."

Cruel Providence

"How do you do, Mr. Shelby? I hope my nephew has not abused of your time and efforts. He is known to be a scoundrel at times, you know."

Earl Hampshire's joviality was certainly contagious. Frank was all smiles. "He hasn't, sir, I can assure you."

"Very well then," Uncle Earl said, returning his attention to William. "You were telling me this journey of yours was not planned."

"I am sorry, for we had not planned a voyage such as this. We simply boarded the first ship and came without much notice. I do apologize for the lack of warning regarding our arrival."

Earl put his hand over William's shoulder before guiding his nephew to the sofas and chairs furnishing the well-appointed parlour. "Yes, my good boy. It is good to have company for we have not had any visitors from England since our own arrival. Have a seat, please. You must be exhausted." Earl pointed to the comfortable sofa.

"Thank you, Uncle. We have come to ask a favour. I do pray you could assist us in this matter." William asked, as the three men sat down.

"Yes, yes of course, son. How could I be of assistance? Are you in some sort of difficulty?"

"No, not at all as such. But we have come to this continent in pursuit of a young lady."

"I thought as much. You have women troubles?" Uncle Earl cut William off while smiling, looking like a strutting peacock. "I have to confess that I do know a little of the womanly plight," he continued, but truly had no idea what was troubling his nephew.

"Yes, Uncle. A woman! However, I am here on account of assisting her for fear she is in grave danger."

"Would you be in great danger also?" Uncle Earl looked much more incredulous with William's last statement.

"No, I do not believe we are. Although, I do not know the extent to which she is at risk either. I have chased Lady Katherin around the globe wanting to free her of what I can only believe is a disastrous situation with the Count of Sussex. He has no virtuous purpose for Lady Katherin, except to hurt her without even as much as offering her any protection. So I must reach out to anyone who has the fortitude to assist in this delicate matter. My purpose is to find her and rescue her from the clutches of the count. Can you help us?" William respectfully requested.

"My dear boy! You can count on my goodwill. Now, pray tell how can I assist you in this endeavour of yours?"

"We will need a place to stay firstly, after which we would need help in locating the passengers who landed shortly before us." William was obviously relieved knowing that his uncle was ready to lend some assistance in his search for Katherin.

"Yes, you may well stay here with our family, of course. It will be most enjoyable to have guests. As for locating the newly disembarked passengers and in turn our quarry in the person of Lady Katherin, would the morrow be soon enough to make a start?"

"Yes, that would be excellent, sir!" William smiled for the first time since meeting his uncle.

"Very well then. But now, my boy, please give me news from England, given that we do not receive much in the way of information?" Uncle Earl asked, manifestly delighted to see his nephew.

Chapter 25

Katherin woke from a nightmare where she dreamt of being held captive with no way out of her confinement. Looking around the room, she found herself alone in a stranger's bed. She felt an overwhelming sense of confusion. What could have happened for her to have been left in this odd place – an inn was it? Katherin had no memory of how she had been transported, or how she was left in this bed, given that she had no recollection of the events that occurred after she was left for dead.

"Oh my dear God!" she said, once she recalled the man who had accosted her and brought her on board the dreadful vessel. No amount of memory loss would help her forget the stench that emanated from the dreadful man either. He had the worst body odour she had ever encountered. Perhaps someone could advise him on his bathing routine for he certainly could benefit from daily ablutions. Although confused and a little disoriented, the idea of being in a strange bed without as much as a memory of how she had landed in it, frightened her. Katherin suddenly heard footsteps in the hall – she froze. However her strong urge to hide was quite compelling, yet she was unable to budge. It was not from being frozen with fright however, but simply from the restraints she had around her wrists and ankles.

"What is this?" she whispered. In her current situation, she decided to lay very still hoping that whoever was walking around in the hall would continue past her room. No, she could hear someone working the key in her door. What next? She pretended to be asleep while praying not to be disturbed further than she had been. She could hear the door opening before it closed again. The foul, insufferable odour that preceded and accompanied its owner reached her nostrils. *My God, what now,* was her immediate thought. She was tied to a bed with him closing in on her. *Had he taken her for himself?* The thought revolted her. It could very well have happened, especially without any recollection of the event. He stopped next to the bed. She had no idea what he was doing; perhaps staring at her for she would not give away that she was awake by opening her eyes. She felt as though she would be sick. Finally she heard him move away from the bed, as his steps were becoming fainter with every stride he took. The door opened once again, and to her relief, she heard it close.

Katherin would have been relieved; except she could not open her eyes for fear that he was still inside the room. She waited for a few minutes before finally hearing more steps in the hallway walking away from the room. It was then that she braved opening one eye before lifting the lid of the other. With no one in sight, she sighed. In her dire circumstance she could not imagine how she was to untie her wrists from the bedposts. She could not reach them to use her teeth to work the knots. What then? She tried to pull up her feet to see whether they were tied as strongly as her wrists were.

"Ah!" she said as she felt one of her restraints around her ankles getting loose. She continued to pull on the rope until her foot broke free from its rope. She worked for quite a while to free the other foot before it too slipped out of the tied loop. It was her wrists that presented a serious challenge. With her legs free, she pulled herself up to use her legs to break the rope that held her hands in place. In spite of her successes, she felt faint with all her struggles and needed to rest before resuming her efforts. Once she could free her hands though, she could figure out what she was doing in this room. However, and once again, she heard footsteps in the hall. She pulled herself flat on her bed in the event that the steps belonged to her kidnapper. She could hear more than one set of footsteps moving toward her room. With panic permeating her entire being, Katherin closed her eyes. Her only wish was to shut out the world and be returned to her family. She could see them. She could watch the children eating at the breakfast table with father sharing his projects for the day with them. She longed to be home. To her relief, she heard the footsteps move away from her room and continue down the corridor.

She continued working on her wrists for another half-an-hour when she finally managed to free her left wrist out of its bonds. It only took seconds to free her right hand. She then raised herself from the bed, when the dizzy spell returned. She sat down again for a minute to steady herself before she got to her feet and rushed for the door. She slowly opened it then looked around for anyone lurking about the corridor. No one was in sight. She made her way down the hallway, stopping at the top of the steps to examine her surroundings. No one was about on the landing below or down the stairs. She descended the stairs slowly, keeping herself poised and alert while she took each step downward. After reaching the bottom, she crossed the floor to exit the inn.

She had no idea which way she should set off, other than she knew she had to escape her captor's hands while the opportunity presented itself. She ran to the side alley, hiding from any onlookers, for she knew not whom she could trust at the moment.

Katherin watched the traffic of horses and carriages traveling to unknown destinations. The streets were thick with mud sticking to the soles of her shoes. She had no choice; she had to make a decision to trust someone. She knew returning to the inn was not a viable option.

When she saw a woman come her way down the footpath she decided to ask for her assistance.

"Excuse me, madam?" she said courteously.

The woman took one look at Katherin and trotted off, obviously disgusted by her appearance.

What was Katherin to do for she had never been in such a dreadful predicament?

"Madam!" she called out once more, but the lady kept rushing away. Knowing full well that she could not remain outside for much longer – the cold was biting at her face and hands – she stood waiting for another pedestrian to come about.

The air was so damp and cold that hypothermia would soon set in if she did not find refuge indoors somewhere close by in the next hour. She stood around for another twenty minutes perhaps before another lady passed by.

She was not as elegant as the last one, but appeared robust; a person who likely worked for a living. Her dress was lovely, almost too brassy. However, Katherin could not think of the kind of occupation a woman might have at this point. She needed help first and foremost. Besides, Katherin, in her adolescent innocence had not been exposed to any inappropriateness to which society would lend itself, and had no preconceived ideas of anything other than the woman being a proper lady.

"Miss, may I ask for your assistance?" Katherin sounded as though she was begging for her next meal while her teeth rattled about her mouth.

"What are you doing out in the cold with not so much as an overcoat, child?" the lady asked, sounding as if she was scolding Katherin.

"I…, I have escaped from a terrible man, who has taken me hostage, Miss," she went on. Only when Katherin heard herself say the words that she knew how ridiculous they must have sounded.

"You certainly do require a warm place. Come with me, child. I will try to help."

Katherin was appreciative of the woman's hospitality of course. "Thank you, ma'am," she said repeatedly.

"Don't thank me yet; you haven't seen my place," she tittered, while taking Katherin's hand and the both of them scurrying down the street. They walked away from the docks for a few minutes, and down a rather dirty street, they entered a building. There was a sign above the door. "Brothel".

"This is what I call home. It's not much better than remaining out in this freezing weather. It will have to suffice though," she told Katherin.

As they climbed the stairs to the woman's apartment, Katherin said, "Thank you for bringing me to your residence, ma'am, but now I must find a way to notify my father."

"Where is your father?" the lady queried, turning the key in the door and opening it.

"He is in London," Katherin stated as a matter-of-factly.

"London? Do you mean London, England?"

"Why yes, do you know where that is?"

"Why I sure do, child!" She laughed heartily, as the two of them entered the room.

"You make fun of me?' Katherin asked, for she was not sure what to make of her new friend's sense of humour.

"No, I am certainly not. My name is Estelle Goodrich," she said, taking her coat and hat off and indicating a chair for Katherin to sit at the table. "You sound like a good child, honey. How is it that you find yourself in America?" she asked.

"I am Katherin Hampton, recently wed to the Count of Sussex, Miss Goodrich," she replied, taking the indicated seat while Estelle hung her coat on the portmanteau by the door.

"Countess, you are then?' Estelle repeated. "And what brings a Countess to America, I can only wonder?"

"I am not sure. As I explained earlier, I was taken from my room in England where I was awaiting the count's return. Before his return, I was taken to a ship and brought here with the promise that the count would soon join us. So, without further explanations, I find myself alone, running from my attacker when, fortunately, you accepted to hear my plea for help."

"Thank you for telling me all this, sweetie, but I do not have a title like yourself. Yet, it does seem that you have had a long difficult journey, and I am not sure what I can do to help. The only girls associated with me are working girls," Estelle admitted, sitting across from Katherin.

"I simply require contacting my father. He would be quite worried."

"I am not certain how we could do that. The ships would take a couple or three weeks to sail back to England, child," she said. Estelle was well aware how the news would affect the young woman. It would probably break the girl's heart. Estelle patted her hand gently and smiled.

Katherin shook her head. "I do understand, Miss Goodrich. But I am not sure where to go in the interim."

"Nor I for that matter. We have to earn our keep to stay here, you see."

"What does a working girl do, Miss Goodrich?" Katherin enquired, lifting her gaze to her new friend.

"We work with men. I don't believe it is the kind of work a countess ought to be doing though. You need more than a delicate constitution to work with the men who frequent our establishment. Possibly, we could locate a relative of yours, or other means for you to board the next ship to England," Estelle offered, not knowing what she was going to do with her latest charge.

"I do not have currency to pay for a passage to England. My father would only be too happy to pay. What ought I to do…?" Katherin stopped short.

She clearly felt like crying from exhaustion, hunger, and beyond assistance. "Should I find a way to send a note to father? He surely would pay for my safe return," Katherin restated.

"We will find a way. Do not worry child. It appears that you could use some clean clothes and perhaps a meal. When was the last time you ate?" Estelle asked.

After looking at Katherin's entire figure, she could tell that the young woman had been through a terrible ordeal.

Following Estelle's scrutinizing glance over Katherin's apparel, she looked at herself and was in disbelief at the sight. For the first time in weeks, she noticed what others saw. In the looking glass across the room, Katherin stared at her reflection. Her hair was dishevelled; her face blackened with dirt and grime, her lips were parched, and bruises decorated her lower arms, wrists and cheeks. She had dark circles under her eyes; her youthful beauty had receded to a past that only memories could conjure up. Katherin resembled a homeless vagabond. She had to agree with Estelle. "I could use a bath and if you could be so kind as to provide some water, it would be most appreciated," Katherin said.

"Let me see what I can do to help." Estelle left the room to arrange for a bath and clean clothes to assist Katherin. Estelle also knew that should she keep Katherin with her, it could be her salvation out of the line of work into which circumstances had forced her.

She was only gone for a very short time when she reappeared in the front room where she had left Katherin. Estelle observed a customer come into the front room and intercepted him before he could accost Katherin.

"I'm afraid the young woman is not available," Estelle said to the man.

"Here is Elsie. She is so very fresh, would you not agree?' Estelle told him, extending a hand in the direction of a woman coming out of her room.

"Yes, thank you, ma'am," the man took off his hat.

"Katherin, come with me," Estelle said, knowing that she could not allow her to roam in the front parlour at leisure. She was clearly too beautiful even under the filth. Estelle brought young Katherin up the long staircase to a room where she asked another young woman to fetch hot water for a bath. Katherin sat down on the bed to undress. She allowed Estelle to assist her, taking off the dirty garments and corset.

Cruel Providence

Once disrobed, she sunk into the hot bath to soothe her bruised and aching body. Estelle then arranged for food to be brought up while she bathed, removing all the dirt from her body and hopefully the memories associated with it.

Given that it had been weeks since Katherin left her father's home, it felt good relaxing in a nice bath.

"I am not as pretty as I once was. My journey across the miles has certainly taken a toll," Katherin explained.

"Not to worry, child. How old are you?" Estelle asked, as she rubbed Katherin's back with a bar of soap.

"I am sixteen," she replied proudly.

"You poor child. Did your father marry you off to this count?"

"Yes, I did not wish to be married, at least not to him!"

"You may be the only woman I've ever encountered that did not wish to marry a count," Estelle admitted giggling.

"You think I should have married him then?"

"Not at all, it's simply a case that most young women aspire to marry such a man, to have a title and power," Estelle said.

"You see, I have met the most handsome, dashing man one could ever meet at the debutante's ball. My heart leapt out of my chest when I laid eyes on him. It was the very same evening my father introduced me to the count. Unfortunately, father made the argument that the count would take better care of my children and me. I wonder how father would take it presently, that is to say should he know how little the count did provide for me?" Katherin said musingly.

"You must have had such a time, Countess," Estelle said ruefully.

"Yes, you may say as much. I would love to be back home with my family."

"You look too young to be married off. Should I have a child your age, I would protect her from the many wolves howling about our home. Was your count an older gentleman?" Estelle queried.

"Yes, he was much older and not as gentle as he professed to be."

Estelle laughed out loud. "You are a treasure, little one. It is a wonder your father could have ever parted with you."

"I would love to be back in father's arms," Katherin said before tears spilled down her cheeks.

"Now, now do not cry, child." Estelle wiped the tears away. "I will promise you that we will find a way to bring you back to England, or my name is not Estelle."

"But you are Estelle, are you not?"

Estelle laughed so hard that everyone in the house could hear her. She then dressed Katherin in a borrowed gown and later brought her some roasted chicken; some potatoes and carrots with some bread and milk. Katherin ate and drank with visible appetite. Afterward she felt much restored. Her ordeal had been a long one.

Chapter 26

William rose early the following morning. He had retired late, but still could not sleep. He dressed and met with his uncle in the front parlour. Since Frank had not appeared thus far, William took the opportunity to speak with his uncle alone.

Earl Hampshire looked a lot like William, although a considerably older version of him. Earl's hair was salt and pepper, receding slightly, and sported a large bushy moustache that was fashionable in the day. He wasn't as tall as his nephew, but his stature was an imposing one. His upper arms attested to hard work.

"Uncle, I do appreciate your goodness of heart. We had no idea this search would take us to the New World when we began our pursuit to locate Miss Katherin. I must confess that she has married Count of Sussex only a few short weeks ago. However, I have it under good authority that she did not wish to marry him, and that the count had married her under less than gentlemanly pretences. Somehow, he had intercepted my arrival at the Hampton's residence to ask for her hand in marriage, deterring his competition. Since that time, we have also learned that he was not honourable when he placed her life in danger by his own admission. Frank and I overheard the count gloating over his deed to rescue Katherin from a villain he had engaged himself. So, this brought us to Boston with little in the way of funds, or news to Katherin's whereabouts," William explained to his uncle as both men sat down for breakfast.

"It sounds as if we have work to do, son. We will find her, that is should she be here. I have many good friends in high places," Uncle Earl stated somewhat proudly.

"Thank you, Uncle Earl. I am very grateful." William was pleased with this new turn of events. Frank Shelby soon joined the men in the parlour.

Frank and William devoured their breakfast with hearty appetite while Uncle Earl ate slightly less than the two young fellows. He had to admire the gumption of youth, the ardour of love and the determination of his nephew in the pursuit of his goal.

"We must set off to claim your young woman," Uncle Earl said to both men once they were replete.

Earl called to have the carriage brought to the front entrance so they could travel to the smoking club near the centre of town. There, Earl would sit down with some of his acquaintances, which he hoped would be instrumental in locating young Katherin Hampton.

Once they arrived, William and Frank were introduced to many of Earl's friends. William was pleased to have been useful in uncovering Katherin's location however, he wished he could move quicker for fear this beautiful young woman was in danger of losing her virtue. He rather wished she were in his arms and not in the arms of the count. William sat as comfortably as possible while listening to the conversations, but felt restless sitting amongst people that may not have any information that proved useful. Frank, too, sat looking around at the guests before asking the servants if there had been any sighting of Miss Katherin Hampton or the Count of Sussex.

While Frank took leave, William remained behind to ask some of the guests, who, by all accounts, were quite talkative with airs that could be construed as snobbish. William could not believe how these pompous men could be so pretentious, for, even in England, you would not see such displays. Nevertheless, William was resigned to accompany his uncle, more to enjoy his support than anything else. If it were not for leads that might come from their efforts, he would have to find other means to obtain information regarding Katherin's whereabouts. Nevertheless, it would be worth socializing for the time being, even though Katherin may very well be in urgent need of his assistance.

A while into the visit at the club, it proved too difficult for William to sit still with the gentlemen smoking and socializing, while laughing, talking, even shouting, as though there was a crisis in the offing. William could not enjoy himself while he knew Katherin was lost and feeling abandoned.

William and Frank decided to meet in the front lobby.

"Frank! Did you gather any news on Miss Katherin?"

"No. I dare say it appears as though no one has set eyes on her. Perhaps we should look outside the plush surroundings of Boston, and visit the less privileged areas of town. She is more likely to be taken where one would not question her abduction," Frank suggested.

"Yes, you may have a good point, Frank."

"We should ask your uncle for directions to this area of town."

"Yes, you make perfect sense as usual."

The two men waited for their opportunity to speak with Earl Hampshire after the social gathering ended.

They were seated in the carriage on their way back to Earl's residence when William spoke.

"Uncle, Frank has pointed out that Miss Katherin may have been brought to an area of Boston that would be more inclined to look the other way when it came to one being abducted. She would more likely to be hidden in such a part of town. Would you not agree?"

"That sounds likely. Good deduction, my boy!" Uncle Earl exclaimed as if they had just discovered America, or something as grand. "Perhaps we will detour our travels to the rundown areas that may be considered the worst of the fair Boston, for you may be absolutely correct, given that not one of my acquaintances has ever heard of her."

The driver was then advised to make a detour to the back streets of Boston. They all were watching through the open windows for any unusual residents, or goings on that they could stop to question. This area reflected the huge differences in the social status of the period. What was obvious was that the rich had located their families in parts of Boston that reflected their social standing, whereas the poor working class had practically nothing to show for their difficult and sometime intolerable existence. Even the houses and local shops within these parts of town were in dire need of repairs. Although, they did not witness any unusual occurrence or notice anything that could be considered a lead toward finding Katherin, Uncle Earl felt they needed to halt their efforts for a moment. He asked his driver to stop so he could enquire from a storekeeper he once knew from an incident that occurred a while ago if the man held any information of Lady Katherin. Earl Hampshire entered the smoke shop and was gone no longer than five minutes when he returned to the carriage to join the young fellows.

William was the first to ask, "Uncle, did the man have any news of Miss Katherin?"

"No, not as of yet. I am sorry, my boy, as it appears she may be more difficult to locate than previously thought, but don't be too worried, for it is only the beginning of our quest."

Chapter 27

Katherin had been asleep when she suddenly heard laughter in another room. This had been the first time since leaving her father's home that Katherin heard amusement from people socializing. She lay on the bed for another half hour, feeling grateful for the rest she so desperately needed. She was very grateful to Estelle for her delightful assistance at a time of great need. Estelle had a sweetness of temper in which Katherin could trust. She had a refreshing demeanour that was most encouraging. What would have become of her should she not have met Estelle? She would make certain that her father compensate Estelle for all her help should Katherin have the chance to see her father again. She longed to be with him as if there were no tomorrow. The thought of never seeing her family again was unbearable. Katherin suddenly heard a knock.

"Yes?" Katherin called out.

"It is Estelle. Miss Katherin, may I come in?" Estelle asked.

"Of course, of course, do come in," Katherin exclaimed.

Estelle entered the room and smiled once she saw Katherin resting in her bed.

"How are you, sweetie?" Estelle sounded genuinely concerned.

"I am feeling much better, and all because of you," Katherin answered, sitting up.

"That is lovely. I wondered if you would like an outing today. We could find something more appropriate for you to wear and book a passage for you on a vessel sailing for England shortly. Would you like that?" Estelle asked.

"That would be excellent, Miss Estelle. However, I do not believe I could board another ship after such an unpleasant voyage. The last passage proved quite difficult on my stomach. Do you suppose I could remain here for a short while until my strength returns? I shan't be in the way," Katherin pleaded.

"Thank you for being honest, my dear. I would love for you to remain here with me, but I do not believe this place is at all suitable for you. We would have to move you elsewhere. I do know of a lady that may be of assistance to take you in until you are strong enough to travel."

"That would be very kind of you. Your kindness is greatly appreciated, and you are not obliged to help me in any manner. You have shown me great kindness and such compassion that I shall not ever forget you." Katherin was very sincere.

"You are such a doll. I would only wish to have a daughter such as you. You are a most measurable find for a young woman causing me to want to do better myself," Estelle went on. She could not believe anyone could cause such pain to someone so gentle. "I want you to dress yourself, then we shall eat out, and celebrate our new friendship. I took the liberty of booking a table at one of Boston's greatest inns. The breakfast there is quite exquisite. After which we will find the most gorgeous dress for you to wear. How does that all sound?"

"Fabulous, though you do understand that I do not have money to pay for such luxuries?" Katherin frowned inquiringly.

"Do not worry." Estelle left the room while Katherin dressed. As soon as she was done, she exited the room to look for Estelle. She readily noted the many ladies sitting around the front room wearing less than discreet attire than what was customary. There were even men sitting around with the ladies, drinking whiskey. She spotted Estelle near the front entrance, quickly walked to her, and they both exited the establishment.

"I do understand what you meant by the place not being quite suitable. I do not understand why you would choose to stay here however?"

"Ah, it is a long story. Some day I may tell you the long of it, but for the moment, let us not speak of it and make unhappy with thoughts of things that cannot be changed. It is such a glorious day that we will have this day for eternity." Estelle did not want to spoil the day with thoughts that brought her back to her own reality. Estelle imagined Katherin being her daughter, and the nice things the two of them would do together. She once had a daughter when she was only seventeen, not much older than Katherin. Her daughter would most likely be the same age as Katherin, that is, if she should be alive today. Estelle, by no means had looked back once she left her baby at the base of the church door one Sunday morning. Estelle could not have kept her, for the cad, who had raped her at sixteen, did not stay to help when she was in desperate need of support. At this time, Estelle felt that having young Katherin to dote upon was her redemption.

They went out to a quaint inn that served a grand meal with both of them eating to their contentment. For Katherin, this had been the best of her travels thus far. It had been too long since she remembered having a more pleasing meal. Estelle lived not very far from this small restaurant but she did not treat herself to such luxury often. Afterwards both women went out to find the most exquisite dress, as Estelle had to return the young woman's dress they had borrowed. They strolled past the small dress shops where Katherin had seen a very attractive blue gown that would be utterly beautiful on her slim figure. Estelle went in the shop ahead of Katherin to purchase the garment.

At the very moment when the two ladies were looking in the window at the dress, William drove past them gazing out for Katherin. William had taken a second look at how the young woman resembled Katherin, but then again he could not believe it to be her. The woman who attracted his attention was attired as a working girl, which Katherin was certainly not. The carriage drove past the woman, leaving Katherin walking into the shop to join Estelle.

The ladies took great pleasure in purchasing the dress, and Katherin looked lovely in it. They had such a grand time that Estelle only wished for the day to last forever. Although Estelle knew she must return to the drudgery of her life, and was soon to deliver Miss Katherin to her good friend, Isabelle Turnkey, Estelle would have loved to stay with Katherin for she had a graceful manner about her that she had not seen for many years.

Miss Isabelle was a simple woman without need of luxuries. Estelle had great hopes that Isabelle would provide Katherin with lodging, as there was no better place for Katherin to remain while in America. Miss Estelle gave the directions to the driver, and asked him to hurry for Estelle required to work this evening. They traveled for no more than a half-an-hour until they were in the country. It was a most beautiful scene teaming with life and new growth within the surrounding trees. They finally pulled up to the tiny residence of Isabelle Turnkey. The coach driver stopped and immediately jumped off to allow Estelle and Katherin to step down from the carriage. Katherin had first seen the cottage style house and thought that perhaps Isabelle Turnkey resided in it only during the summer months for it appeared too small to live permanently in such a small residence. Katherin had been accustomed to living in a large estate; only knowing the wealthy residences of England provided her with a very narrow view of the world. It seemed preposterous for someone to live in such a small dwelling.

Estelle introduced the two ladies. Soon both women seemed quite comfortable with one another. Not long afterward, Miss Estelle departed rather quickly, making her excuses.

In the beginning, Miss Katherin felt slightly awkward with being left behind so hastily, but soon found that Miss Turnkey was extremely kind. They entered the small dwelling, which Katherin could see was well maintained, looking as though Isabelle took excellent care of her home. They both sat at the table where Isabelle brought tea for Katherin. While talking they began to get to know one another with Isabelle asking a few questions. She could see by Katherin's appearance, along with her posture that she had been well educated and had benefited from the best upbringing. However, Isabelle could not imagine why Katherin was sitting in her parlour and not with her own family. These days no one in their right mind would allow a refined woman, who appeared to be of a delicate constitution, to travel alone so far from home. Could the girl be in some kind of trouble? Estelle had not divulged much by way of an explanation as to why Miss Katherin required a place to stay while in America.

"I am very pleased to have you stay with me, Miss Katherin. May I ask the reason for coming to America and why you should agree to lodge in my cottage?" Isabelle questioned, obviously puzzled.

"It appears that staying with Miss Estelle would not be proper. I was therefore ushered to stay with you so that I have a proper place to reside before returning to England. I did not feel strong enough to travel back to England so soon. I hope this will not inconvenience you?"

"I did not know you were so far from home, my dear. You must be very lonely?" Isabelle said, sipping on her tea.

"I am definitely longing for home. I did not want to leave father's residence at all."

"What was it that made you leave then, child?"

"My father had the notion I would greatly benefit from marrying the Count of Sussex for he wanted my hand in marriage," Katherin admitted with a grief-stricken face.

"Then where is the count?" Isabelle enquired, even more curious now.

"I do not know. We were in this tiny English inn when the count left on some urgent matter. He did not return but someone was sent in his stead. Regrettably, this man took me on board a ship while promising that the count would soon join us, and for whatever reason, he did not appear. I knew not what I should do, for this brute of a man had locked me in a room below deck. He brought me to this country after traveling for days on end. I do not travel well on board a ship."

"You do look like you could put on a little weight, my dear girl. Would you care for some sweet cakes?" It was obvious to Isabelle that the dark circles around Katherin's eyes and gauntness proved somehow that she had been starved. Isabelle pushed the sweets in front of Katherin.

"Ah yes, they look terribly delicious. Did you bake them yourself, Miss Isabelle?" Katherin could not resist her sweets, although it hadn't been long since she last ate. By this time Katherin was malnourished and lacking energy.

"Yes, I did. Do you like them?"

"Oh yes! They are so full of flavour. Do you bake for a living?"

"No, but I shall bake some more if you are very fond of them. Could I get you some milk with the sweets? I only have goat's milk."

"That would be delightful, thank you. You mustn't get up. Allow me to retrieve the milk. I would not want you to bake any more sweets. You should rest with me so I can have the pleasure of your company. You are so very kind to allow me to stay with you and I cannot think how I may repay you for your kindness."

They chatted through the remainder of the day. It was becoming rather late when Miss Isabelle prepared a small meal before retiring for the night. She showed Katherin her room, and mentioned that if the next day would be pleasant outdoors, they would go for a walk to the market to fetch the needed staples.

"Do you not have a carriage?" Katherin could not help but ask.

"Yes, my dear. It is simply more pleasurable to walk in the fresh air."

"I am not sure; I have not had the pleasure to do so."

"You have missed out on such fine and pleasant walks. I bid you goodnight, my dear," Isabelle said before retiring.

"Goodnight, Miss Isabelle, and I thank you from the bottom of my heart for your generosity. I will also speak with father so that he will compensate you as well as Miss Estelle."

"You are a dear girl. No need to compensate anyone for your pleasure is ours. Wherever have you come from, you would do well to have touched the many lives with your good heart."

"I thank you. What a kindred soul you are. Miss Estelle was so very kind, too. Thank you both," Katherin said.

Isabelle smiled at Katherin. "It is no wonder Miss Estelle had a special spot in her heart for you," Isabelle repeated before saying, "Goodnight, dear," and then closed her bedroom door behind her.

In the meantime, the horrid Mr. Cathers had continued to seek Katherin's whereabouts. He had been quite hot tempered after discovering his captive missing. He questioned the innkeeper for any clues to her whereabouts, although it did not prove to be of any use.

"Mr. Cathers, we have not seen the young woman you refer to since the evening you booked the room. You might keep a closer eye on your so-called daughter the next time. If I remember correctly, she was rather intoxicated when you first brought her in. Perhaps she went in search of another tavern to drink herself to sleep," the innkeeper suggested.

"Yee prove no help at all!" Mr. Cathers said. "I'd be takin' leave," he announced before paying his bill.

"Surely, but that will be fifty cents sir," the innkeeper stated.

"For a night. That's robbery," he bellowed.

Mr. Cathers threw the money on the counter and left the inn. He had become quite unruly after he realized that most of his cash from the count had been spent. And without Katherin to deliver to his associate, Mr. Cathers was in great need of money to continue his travels. He had to find her quickly. She could not have gotten far in her condition. He would ask in town for surely someone had noticed a young woman walking about in a gown with temperatures still dipping below freezing at night.

Chapter 28

While all of this was occurring in Boston, Mr. Edward Hampton had returned to England. Today, he was preparing to travel to the city to hire a local detective. He could not help but think how he should have listened to Katherin. Perhaps she did know what was best after all. He had raised all his children to think for themselves and to trust their hearts as their mother had instilled in them. Should Constance be with him at this moment, she would have prevented the count from marrying their daughter, saving this whole travesty from happening. Where could Katherin be? Mr. Hampton had no idea. Whereas a detective would surely be capable of finding out what happened to Katherin. He did have an inkling that she may have boarded a ship heading for the Americas, but without proof he could not be certain. The detective would determine whether she had crossed the ocean or not. He had been told the ships would take approximately three weeks to reach the Americas, and of course only if the vessel would meet with propitious weather conditions. Could he remain waiting for a reply at the very least two months before word would reach his ears in England? Mr. Hampton would have liked to travel himself, yet he had the other children to consider. And, of course, his work had already suffered in his absence. Therefore, his choice was to remain at home, as it made the most practical sense. He could then send word with the detective to give to a distant cousin of his, who may prove quite helpful in the search for Katherin.

After the long drive into the city, Mr. Hampton met with the detective in question. They came to an agreement. All the information Mr. Hampton could possibly provide would be useful, whereas any information withheld may prove to be detrimental in solving the riddle of Katherin's disappearance. He could only pray for her safe return. And with some last words to Mr. Murphy, Edward returned home.

After he had resolved this matter, he began to feel pain in his chest. He had no idea whether the pain was due to grief, or something more urgent. He surely had his fair share of sorrow recently; perhaps it was taking a toll on his health. In the latter part of the evening, he asked Miss Louise to summon the doctor, as the pain had not abated. He knew he could not leave his children orphans, even if he desired to be with his beautiful wife. The doctor arrived within a few hours, and they both talked about his ongoing health concerns. The physician took all the necessary information while making his diagnosis.

"At present, I would like you to take these herbs for the pain, or whenever you feel tightness in your chest. You will have to relax; otherwise, you will cause damage to your heart should you continue to manage your daily routine in such a fashion. I am not certain the pain you experience emanates from your heart, however. Chest pain could be caused by a variety of different reasons such as indigestion. For the present moment however, you should take it easy."

"Thank you," Edward Hampton said, "and I will relax. I would not want this pain to return. It was good of you to come by at this late hour."

After the doctor left the Hampton's residence, Miss Louise came down to the study and scolded him.

"You ought to know, Miss Louise, that your scolding is causing me some undue stress. I would be obliged for you to put an end to your reproach."

"Of course! I should not want to cause you more pain. I apologize for my rudeness," Miss Louise said, before leaving the room to fetch some water for the patient. She soon returned with water and gave him the powdered herbs the doctor had left for him to take.

At the moment, Miss Louise had her hands full, for she not only cared for the ever-growing needs of the children, but presently her employer had fallen ill. She hoped that he would recover from his ordeal. He had not entirely recovered emotionally from losing his wife. What's more he was blaming himself for Miss Katherin's disappearance. Thus, Miss Louise vowed to help Mr. Hampton through this dark time, which was likely the cause of his current illness. Besides, she was not willing to lose yet another employer.

It was no wonder Miss Louise had never married, with little time for herself; she would not have had the time to care for yet another family. She wondered whether someday she would regret her decision to remain a spinster, but felt quite content caring for the Hampton's children.

"Mr. Hampton, have you received any news regarding Miss Katherin?"

"No, I cannot say that I have, at least not as of yet, although I have employed a detective to follow her trail," Mr. Hampton replied.

"I understand, and pray tell who is this detective?"

"His name is Mr. Alexander Murphy. I have been told he is an excellent choice. Why do you ask?"

"I have heard that Mr. Murphy was very good at uncovering truths, Mr. Hampton," Miss Louise said.

"Yes! I have it in good authority that Mr. Murphy is a great detective. With any luck, we will have Katherin returning home before long."

"This would be delightful, Mr. Hampton. The children miss her greatly. Now I would like for you to rest. We do not want more trials here at the house," she said firmly, before leaving the room where Edward Hampton was beginning to feel drowsy.

Edward had to agree with his governess. There had been too much chaos for one family to endure. He vowed that he would not allow more unpleasant circumstances to affect the family. In spite of the state of his present business affairs, he would have loved to embark on a trip to the Americas. It was once his dream to take a long voyage, although under the present circumstances, he could not see himself traveling. He had carried out his duty to care for his children, or he did his best, and perhaps would have been quite different should he not have loved Constance.

Mr. Murphy was on the first ship out of Southampton. He had not wasted much time once he had been engaged other than a day to find Miss Katherin's trail to the Americas. He felt confident he could locate the lovely young woman. This he believed would be his easiest assignment to date. He simply would follow her to America, locate her, and bring her home to Mr. Hampton at once, receiving a very large sum to allow him to retire. He had only to endure approximately a month of travel aboard a ship for he would be relaxing for part of his travels.

Chapter 29

Estelle was rather pleased with the way she performed the night before with her customers. They came in steadily during the past evening. At this rate, she would have enough saved to retire in the very near future. Apart from wanting to see how Miss Katherin was getting along with Isabelle, Estelle did not mind working some extra hours. Perhaps she would journey out to her friend's cottage near the end of the week after the customers were less frequent, that is; when the ships sail out of the harbour. Estelle had been not more than Katherin's age when she was brought to America with great hopes of finding a rich man to marry with whom she could settle down. She could have conceivably raised a whole brew of children. She found her dreams were quickly dashed soon after she landed on the shores of the New World. There were no rich men as had been told there would be. And marriage simply was not an option, for she only found positions that were extremely demanding, and sailors, who did frequent the port for short stays. Seamen were not willing to marry either. Money being scarce, while sailors plentiful, Estelle's days soon drew into weeks, followed by months of scraping the bottom of the barrel, as it were, with little to pay for life's necessities. She was not finding the means to easy cash, and undemanding occupation did not come easily either. Nor did she wake up one fine morning with aspirations to become a working girl, for her dreams were more to sing on a stage and success would hence follow. On the other hand, her dreams were not fulfilled, and she found herself destitute, alone, with no one to help with her aspirations to be on stage.

This seemed a lifetime ago, but young Katherin brought not only a breath of fresh air, but also her unfulfilled dreams of being someone respectable. Katherin reminded Estelle of how she was once innocent and full of dreams of making it in the New World that now seems gone insane. And here was a beautiful young woman, who marries a count only to run from him for God only knew why. She had to give Katherin credit for following her heart, however. She must have endured a great deal, for one had to take a good look at Katherin to see how she had suffered at the hands of the swine. But still she kept her innocence. *Good for her,* Estelle thought. But Estelle knew she wasn't as brave as Katherin for when time became relatively difficult, Estelle offered herself to men. She felt she had nothing to lose, apart from the savage rape she had endured at a young age of fifteen, and where she became pregnant. Once she had the child, she had no virtue to save, and thus, she was passed on from one man to another. She would not allow this to happen to Katherin, which further motivated her to protect the young countess's virtue at all cost.

Estelle had become aware that there was a man asking about a young woman with Katherin's description, and they were able to divert him off her scent for the present time. Nevertheless, she had no idea whether the other women for a small fee would divulge information to the stranger. Estelle worried that some of the women could not be trusted. She would ask around at once, although she did not want to give too much away. She would be extra careful when she traveled to check on Katherin and Isabelle later that week to ensure Katherin's safety.

It was at Isabelle's cozy cottage that Katherin felt somewhat safe since her ordeal began, and not simply from the elements, but also from Mr. Cathers. She was beginning to wonder whether all men were to be distrusted. The days went by easily for Isabelle was quite busy teaching Katherin the use of a variety of herbs and tea leaves. She also taught her how to bake sweets. Katherin would never have been trained in the culinary arts at home; they had a cook to look after such functions. Katherin quite enjoyed learning the art of baking, for this art might come quite handy some day.

"Miss Isabelle, do you not have cooks to take care of your baking needs?" Katherin asked when she first began to help Isabelle in her baking endeavour.

"No! I have no need of a cook. I love to bake," had been her response.

"I had not known the pleasures of baking, for our cook does all the necessary food preparations. Miss Louise would not instruct the children in the art of cooking. It rather seemed redundant to educate them in the performance of any menial tasks. She designed her lessons around the skills deemed appropriate for an accomplished lady, or gentleman."

"That is fine for some people. I much prefer to know what goes into my cooking," Isabelle said with a smile that gave away her true intent – she simply wanted to do it all for herself.

"You tease me, do you not?"

"Yes. You must realize that there are many different roles one must play in the world. Some people have cooks and governesses, whereas some live a much simpler life, and that is just fine according to them."

"I do understand, although our family is rather privileged."

"I would like you to think about this. Does it mean some are privileged when they never have learnt an art? Or would it be fair to say one is privileged to learn an art such as baking? Who is the one receiving more?"

"I do see your point. I had not thought of this twist. It does make perfect sense. Perhaps, it is not so much as a privilege or less, but rather advantages of learning a craft. So you learned the art of baking, and one can see you love to do so, as this is obvious with the beautiful results of your sweets. Whereas another person such as Miss Estelle loves her, what was it she mentioned? Ah yes, she is a workingwoman! What exactly is a working girl?"

"We shan't get into that subject today for that would consist of another topic all together." Isabelle laughed.

"So be it then. I do believe I quite understand you."

Katherin remained with Isabelle Turnkey for several weeks, benefiting greatly from her education and wisdom. Katherin took to Isabelle like a duck took to water. With Isabelle being warm and sensitive, it sent enduring feelings of being loved, which Katherin had missed for the past couple of years. As for Isabelle, helping Katherin filled a void in her life left by the absence of her own mother. It remained a mystery why Isabelle would stay so isolated from the world, when clearly she possessed the qualities to help others become skilled in various tasks. Then again Isabelle seemed not to be affected from the seclusion.

It wasn't long before the days soon stretched into weeks. One day, a gentleman came calling at the cottage. Katherin did not recognize the visitor. *Perhaps it was a good friend of her companion Miss Isabelle,* Katherin thought. She was outdoors gathering a variety of herbs and flowers when the stranger came over to the small dwelling. He walked up the path toward the house.

"How do you do, Miss? Would this be the residence of Miss Isabelle Turnkey?" he asked Katherin.

"Why yes!"

"Could I have a word with her?"

"If you would kindly wait here, I will look inside?"

"Yes, thank you," the gentleman replied, bowing respectfully to Katherin.

Seconds later Isabelle called out to him: "May I help you?" from the small window in her kitchen.

"Yes, ma'am. Might I take up a moment of your time?"

She exited the home to speak with the man. "Would you go inside, dear," Isabelle asked Katherin, as she waved her towards the entrance. "What can I do for you, sir?"

"I have come a great distance, sailing from England. I am providing Mr. Edward Hampton some services. He wishes for me to return his daughter to his estate in England, ma'am. I do believe Lady Katherin, Countess of Sussex, nee Katherin Hampton has been residing with you. Would that be the young lady who went inside?" he asked.

"How would I know whether you are genuine, Mr...?"

"I am extremely sorry, ma'am. Do accept my apologies. I am Mr. Alexander Murphy. As I mentioned, I am in the employ of Mr. Edward Hampton."

"You claim her father sent you to find Miss Katherin?"

"Yes, ma'am."

"Father sent you?" Katherin called out from the kitchen window.

"Quite sure. Are you Lady Katherin, nee Katherin Hampton then, Miss?"

"I am most certainly, Mr. Murphy!" Katherin stated excitedly.

"Thank you, Lady Katherin for being honest. Your father, Mr. Hampton has sent for you all the way from England. He was most troubled with your disappearance. He will be extremely grateful for your safe return."

"I am so very pleased! All along I had known father would not have forgotten me, just as I have told Miss Isabelle here. Didn't I, Miss Isabelle?"

"You sure did, dear child, you sure did." Miss Isabelle was on the verge of shedding a tear. She was happy for Katherin on the one hand, yet, on the other, the world without her would be quite different now – perhaps unbearable at times.

Chapter 30

In the very beginning, William had been quite hopeful in locating Katherin. Unfortunately he had not found any evidence of her being in America. He had searched incessantly for the few weeks and could not be more disappointed with his results. Today, with a very heavy heart, he was to sail on the *Mayfair* once again, to return to England. While crossing the street to begin boarding, he happened to witness what appeared to be a young woman arguing with a gentleman, which caught his attention.

At first he thought he was having some sort of vision due to fatigue. But no, that wasn't it. The lady who had caught his eye was indeed Miss Katherin Hampton.

He had found her at long last, except that it appeared as if she was in dire need of assistance yet again. It soon became evident that the gentleman was manhandling her, but she was fighting back. William ran over to offer his help, although could not reach her before a second man approached them both.

Mr. Murphy came between Katherin and Mr. Cathers. Mr. Cathers had forcefully taken hold of her arm before demanding that Mr. Murphy give her up with the claim that he had prior ownership of the girl. Both men argued while William reached the trio. As he came to stand beside Katherin, Mr. Cathers pulled out a dagger. What appeared to be a knife intended for Mr. Murphy merely became one directed at William. When William backed away from the two men with the dagger sticking out from his side, it was clear that Mr. Cathers' knife had found flesh to cut.

"Mr. Hampshire!" Katherin shouted. Nevertheless, in the ensuing chaos, the diversion enabled Mr. Murphy to run off with Katherin and board their ship.

In the distance, Frank had observed the commotion that resulted in mayhem, although he arrived much too late to be of any great assistance. William was already on the ground bleeding profusely from his side. Frank Shelby rushed to help his friend and watched as Mr. Cathers ran after Katherin, who was screaming at the top of her lungs. Frank knelt by William's side only to hear him shout for Frank to run after Katherin. After Frank placed his scarf on William's wound, he obliged and ran after her. Mr. Murphy and Katherin had already boarded the Mayfair when Frank caught up with Mr. Cathers.

They both fought with their foils drawn while the ship Katherin boarded sailed off. It was a good fight for both men had their advantages; one being older and more experienced, while the other had his youth to dodge the opponent's epee swiftly. Passengers on board watched the fight and heard the clanging of the foils hitting one another and were delighted to witness the unfolding events. When Frank backed away from the charging Mr. Cathers, he found Frank's epee piercing his heart. In shock, Mr. Cathers fell to the ground with a look of total surprise on his face. Frank at once called out to William.

At the moment, Earl Hampshire was on his way to say farewell to his nephew. Frank joined William and called Earl to assist with William's inauspicious accident.

Earl Hampshire immediately summoned for help. Frank found military soldiers in red coats surrounding them. They were about to arrest the assailant, but who was not clear. At the height of the chaos no one was entirely sure how it all began or why. Fortunately, one officer, who had witnessed the duel between Frank and Mr. Cathers, had come forth to argue that the swine lying dead had planted his dagger into William's side – "totally unprovoked reaction," he explained. Thus, no criminal actions could be brought against Frank.

Mr. Hampshire had words with the military superior, who helped Frank pick William's unconscious body up to transport him to Mr. Hampshire's residence. After Frank hailed the first carriage, they departed quickly. Earl Hampshire would ensure that his physicians return William to health – at least he was hopeful this would be possible, for the gash in his nephew's side was deep.

Meanwhile, Katherin had witnessed much of what had transpired and began to cry in Mr. Murphy's arms. Her tears were for William, of course. She dearly wanted to be with him, even at the risk of not sailing to England where her father would be waiting for her. She could not endure the thought of losing William again, for he was clearly lying on the docks alone, most likely dying from his wounds. How could Mr. Murphy be so cruel as to leave him lying in a pool of blood? Katherin could not comprehend.

The Mayfair sailed onward to the English shores with Katherin. She could not be consoled and erupted in hysteria on the decks for everyone to witness.

Katherin had sobbed herself to sleep many nights during their voyage. Meanwhile, what became of great concern was her health. She did not fare well traveling by sea, falling quite ill immediately after departure. She suffered terribly from the waves that never ceased to pulsate, as though the sea was a breathing entity. The violent seas made travel gruelling. Mr. Murphy had plenty to keep himself occupied while tending to Katherin, for he had not known how difficult it could be to travel with such a frail young woman. Katherin protested at every suggestion he gave her. She was obviously upset with the aggravation of leaving after she finally found William.

Katherin had repeatedly dreamed of William since last seeing him. Her dreams were what provided her the steam to push forward when she could no longer bear the pain and suffering she underwent with seasickness. Katherin fell into a tragic state of despondency.

Chapter 31

The voyage to England was almost as brutal as the trip to America with one exception, the absence of Katherin's brutal captor. However, Katherin was in mourning for yet another loss in her life. She had come to believe that she would never love anyone seeing that they certainly perished soon after she became attached to them. Katherin was resigned to be happy to live a sedentary life for the remainder of her days as Isabelle had done, and never leave the sanctuary of the Hampton's estate. She would wear black for the next year and perhaps longer, since she would want everyone to know how she dearly mourned the deaths of her beloved.

Mr. Murphy had made sincere efforts to console Katherin, but he felt at a loss to make a difference, as she would not make it easy. She refused to eat, and when she tried, she could not keep it down, and walking about the ship proved unsafe for she would faint. Mr. Murphy had never earned his living in such an honest way. It took every ounce of effort to secure his reward because should she die before they arrived on solid ground, he would not be in any receipt of cash awards whatsoever. He not only wanted his reward, but he sincerely shared in Miss Katherin's pain. After traveling with her and once she had calmed down, she was quite agreeable. He had been touched by her sincere loving heart and truly knew she was one of a kind from which fairy tales were created. If he ever had a choice for a child, *let it be someone like Miss Katherin,* he thought. He presently understood her father's desperation to find his daughter. What brought Mr. Hampton to give his daughter's hand in marriage to someone like a ruthless count was beyond his capable intellect to comprehend. She was breathtaking to look upon. Even though she was gravely ill, her silken skin had retained the softness of ivory. Her hair was a radiant and brilliantly sun-spun colour that could not be reproduced on any portrait, and her delicate figure was divine. They were not far from port when the captain announced one more day before arriving. It was actually one day earlier than expected. The captain had made headways with southwestwardly winds that pushed them ever so swiftly towards the shores of England. The travelers were thankful for it, no doubt.

Miss Katherin had only ceased being ill in the last few days. She was now managing a little bread when she received word of their imminent arrival. This alone had encouraged her to live for it would not be very long before she could walk on firm ground with legs that were steady; and not forget the motivating force of seeing her sisters and brother for whom she longed incessantly now. They most assuredly had grown since Katherin last seen them. The only thought that bothered her was the count, and how she would have to convince her father never to let him see her again. She would agree to live in seclusion for her sacrifice, as she would not be able to survive living with a man who would have allowed someone like Mr. Cathers to take her away as he did. This alone must be cause to seek estrangement from a man, who clearly should have protected her, but instead left her to die. She felt confident her father would be sympathetic to her pleas.

The ship finally pulled into Southampton. Katherin could now see the island of which she swore never to leave again. The only sorrows she would have was not to see Miss Isabelle or Miss Estelle, for they had shown kindness that she had not seen since leaving home. The other reason she felt extremely sorrowful was for William lying on the docks with blood oozing from his side, which image would linger in her memory until the day she left this good earth. She felt terrible to have to leave him in such a state without as much as a goodbye, or tell him how much she loved him. Never to have closure by attending his funeral would be very regrettable. Certainly she would contact his family to inform them of his unexpected and unfortunate demise.

Currently, she was becoming excited to leave the ship and return home to enjoy her family's presence. At least one dream would come true. She could see the docks as they approached the shoreline, and seeing the dock workers and waiting families walking about the pier was a most delightful experience. She would soon be part of that world again; a world that could appreciate the scenery of the most magnificent country, displaying colours that nature had painted on its canvas. After docking, they both got off the ship once it was securely moored and the gangway lowered to the pier. Mr. Murphy had secured a carriage to take them to the Hampton's estate. The ride to her home, however felt incredibly long, as Miss Katherin had built up the anticipation of being greeted by her family with embraces and kisses. It was clear that she adored them.

At long last, they turned the final corner, beginning their long drive to her home. Katherin had looked on at the beautiful gardens that surrounded the estate with a splendid array of colours that seem to be parading by the carriage window. The grounds were decorated with an array of flowering shrubs and flowers. Everything was more beautiful than she remembered. She could smell the fragrances that she felt would never again encumber her memory after leaving her home so many months ago. Katherin felt her ordeal had come to a closing chapter, as the carriage pulled in front of the mansion.

Katherin was so impatient to be helped out the carriage that she was opening the door before the driver had a chance to reach it. She desperately wanted to be inside with her family, who would be incredibly delighted to see her. The butler opened the door and looked very surprised to see Miss Katherin standing on the stoop. He smiled and would have announced her arrival, except Miss Katherin had run ahead rushing past him to seek out her father.

She opened the door of the den wide and saw her father seated at his big oak desk.

As Edward Hampton's gaze rested on her, he was overcome with incredulity.

He blinked once for it was surely an apparition of his beautiful daughter. When she did not disappear however, he smiled while finding his voice.

"My dear girl, is it truly you?" he bellowed, standing up and rounding his desk.

"Papa!" Katherin returned before she crossed the floor in as little steps as she could muster. It was likely the most unladylike action she had ever done in his presence. They both embraced and looked at one another repeatedly with a sense of disbelief before he spoke. "My dear girl, you are home. I am so very pleased! Will you ever forgive me?" he pleaded while Katherin could not push away from his embrace.

"Father, I do forgive you, but truly there is nothing for you to be upset. I am so pleased to be back with you. I did not know if I could ever find my way home. It is truly a miracle thanks to Mr. Murphy. I must apologize to him, for I am being forgetful of my manners. Father, Mr. Murphy," she turned to show Mr. Murphy into the den.

"Yes, thank you, Miss Katherin. You do not have anything for which to apologize. I am extremely delighted to be able to reunite you with your family," the detective declared.

"Mr. Murphy, you have my deepest gratitude," Mr. Hampton said.

"Do sit down, Mr. Murphy. Katherin, would you seek out your brother and sisters to surprise them as well. They will not believe your presence being possible, and I am quite certain that they will not be able to study once they lay eyes on you.

"But first, I must conclude my business with Mr. Murphy before we begin our celebrations for your safe return."

"Thank you, Papa. I am so very excited to see them, may I be excused?" Katherin quickly exited the room and ran up the stairs. She seemed to have recovered from her illness the moment she passed the threshold of her home, and with lightness of foot, she climbed the staircase. She knocked ever so lightly on the door where the children would surely be. No answer. She again knocked with more force for Miss Louise would indeed hear the knock.

"Come in!" Miss Katherin heard.

Katherin opened the door to see her siblings seated quietly at their tables, listening to what appeared to be a lesson in geography. They could not have grown much in such a short time, could they? Then they finally reacted by screaming Katherin's name. They all bolted towards her. Miss Louise, too, was extremely pleased to see Katherin. She afforded a smile to show her emotions.

Later that same evening, her father informed Katherin that the count had encountered an unexpected end. He recounted the events that occurred when he arrived in France to seek the count. He explained the reason for challenging the man in a duel, which began at midday. The judge had ensured that both were holding only one epee since no other weapons were allowed. They both took ten steps forward, and once at the count of ten, they turned facing their opponent to begin the fencing duel. The count had come forth quickly, taking Mr. Hampton by surprise, as he was not accustomed to such a charge. However rushed he felt, Mr. Hampton had raised his foil to protect himself. They both fought well with their epees clanging continuously. It appeared that they were both well matched in the art of fencing. Mr. Hampton was undoubtedly beginning to tire, for his breathing was erratic and proving to be difficult. However, he did not falter in the least for he continued to meet the count's strokes of the foil equally. Finally, the count came rushing at Mr. Hampton, where he turned away quickly, backing the count into a wall with nowhere to escape. Mr. Hampton positioned his sword directly into the count's chest. The count gave a deafening cry as his eyes looked enormous. Mr. Hampton had never caused injury to anyone before that day, let alone the death of anyone. Therefore, he felt remorse when he witnessed the count bent over in pain. The judge rushed to the count's side. However, the next minute came as a most surprising scene. The count reached into his vest, pulling out a knife out of it. He inserted the small knife into Mr. Hampton's upper shoulder.

Cruel Providence

The judge separated the two men for the count had instantly forfeited the outcome of the duel while breaking the law. He had acted out of hate and loathing for Mr. Hampton. Hence a doctor was summoned to the room. Later that day the count died from his injuries. Katherin was surprised for she thought her father was about to announce William's death. It was of great relief to Katherin, and presently she was discharged of any connection with the count, since their marriage had been annulled forthwith.

After recounting the events that occurred in France, Katherin shared her story of William and how deeply she would miss him.

Mr. Hampton, in his turn, became concerned for Katherin's health. He thus summoned the family physician to the Hampton's home. When the doctor arrived, he found that Katherin was rather weak, but would be restored to health as soon as she began eating properly and given that she was now surrounded by the love of her family.

Once everything had returned to normal, the Hamptons announced a celebration in the next few weeks after Katherin had regained her strength.

The time for the social event Mr. Hampton had arranged for Katherin finally approached. Many invited guests were to visit the family home, which had not seen so many guests in a long time. The children were extremely joyful ever since Katherin had come home. As for Katherin, she was pleased, although she seemed out of sorts somehow. Her father could see how she had grown during the past few months. She had traveled the globe and perhaps had seen in excess of the world at such a tender age. Mr. Hampton did not know if he would ever forgive himself for what had caused his eldest so much pain, but he knew she had forgiven him. Still, he promised to have a father-daughter private conversation once the celebration was over.

After the guests arrived at the reunion ball, the evening proceeded with dancing and gay partying as the guests settle into what appeared to be a delightful time. The evening was uneventful for most part of the night. There were many close friends and acquaintances of the Hamptons in attendance enjoying the festivities. With the evening winding down and guests beginning to disperse, some leaving around midnight, Mr. Hampton announced he could not keep his surprise much longer. He would certainly burst from restraining himself. It was then that Miss Katherin was brought to the front of the ballroom with her eyes covered with a blindfold.

Katherin was very excited, for she could not imagine what her father's surprise could possibly be. Perhaps he had commissioned a portrait of her mother, or maybe of herself. Her father escorted Katherin to the front of the room where he pulled the blindfold from in front of her eyes.

"Oh my!" Katherin was utterly speechless.

"Katherin, please do say what you feel. Are you not pleased?" her father asked.

"Are you not well, my dear girl?"

"Yes, Father..., quite sure!" She finally breathed these words once she had found her voice.

"I wanted to surprise you, not frighten you to death," he insisted.

"I am incredibly surprised. Could this be true?" She found herself blinking to see whether this was perhaps an illusionary trick, or was she actually seeing the man of her dreams.

"Mr. William Hampshire!" she stammered, utterly baffled.

"We have surprised you then. Mr. Hampshire's presence is the result of Mr. Murphy's good deed. He kindly invited Mr. Hampshire to our celebration. He explained the entire story. My only wish was for you to be well and home once again," Edward Hampton stated, not knowing whether he had done something noble for her reaction was of total dismay.

"I am so very pleased, Papa. Thank you, and for you to come to the celebration this good evening," Katherin said to William.

William, still recovering from his wounds, stated, "If it were not for Mr. Murphy overhearing you while you were with fever on board the Mayfair, we would not have known your heart's true desire."

"Mr. Murphy had made certain to locate Mr. Hampshire in Boston for this celebration to be so outstanding," Mr. Hampton added.

Katherin had been dreaming of having Mr. Hampshire by her side. Disbelief that the evening events were actually occurring crossed her mind several times. She was utterly in awe! How could this be happening? Could dreams come true?

It turned out that Mr. Hampshire was Lord William Alexander Hampshire of Newcastle. Mr. Hampton had no inkling it was the one and only Lord of Newcastle. It was true that he had recently inherited his new title with the passing of his elderly father. He was likely the richest man in all of England. Mr. Hampton was originally not interested in pairing his daughter with William; mainly believing that the count would be a preferable suitor in protecting her, along with assisting him financially during his dire circumstance. Should he have looked closer at the count's details, he would have found out that he was not as prosperous as what was purported. Edward Hampton would have been against his daughter marrying such a blighter. Edward Hampton would have done right by Katherin by marrying her to a man she loved. William would certainly protect her as he had shown in the past few months. This was all Mr. Hampton could have hoped for, that is to have his daughter married to the one she loved and desired.

Chapter 32

"I would like you to come back to the present day where you are relaxed, and lying down on the sofa in my office. When I count to three you will open your eyes. One, two, three, you can open your eyes now," Professor Brown ordered.

Jewel Seymour slowly opened her eyes. The glaring lights were too bright at first. She blinked, closing her eyes before they could adjust her sight to the lights. In the beginning, she found herself confused. Her surroundings were obviously very different than the life she had witnessed in the past while.

The professor was staring directly in her eyes, looking for signs of being coherent with her settings.

"Are you all right?" Professor Brown asked, looking quite concerned for his patient. "Perhaps, I've taken you to the 18th century a little too long," he said.

"No, I was caught in the moment. It was difficult to come back. It all appeared so real, as though I was actually back in that era. How long was I under?" Jewel asked.

"It did last over six hours, which was unusually long for a hypnotic session. I tried to bring you out several times, but clearly you required being under for the entire duration of your regression. You must have had to come back at a much happier time in your life," Professor Brown said, not knowing what else would explain her reluctance to return.

"I see. Did you record the entire session?"

"Yes, it's all recorded and will be available for you to review."

"Might we try again sometimes soon? I believe I have learnt details that will help me through this lifetime, like my fears of being helpless or wanting to be in control. And simply knowing myself on a deeper level would be quite beneficial."

"Why yes we can try again, but let's take a break before we try again."

"That would be alright. Let me buy you dinner tonight, and we can meet here for another session in a week or so perhaps, that is if you don't mind?"

"No, not at all, dinner sounds great!" the professor agreed.

At dinner, the professor continued questioning Jewel looking for information that may be pertinent to his unusual hypnotic session, perhaps gaining valuable information for his research.

"Did you feel at any time that you were in danger?"

"I did, but for reasons that I cannot fully explain, it felt as though it was real yet not unlike watching a movie that was so intense that you sit at the edge of your seat," Jewel said. "In the 18th century, women had very little say regarding their lives. Nowadays, women take for granted things such as marriage, careers, and earning potential. Having control over their own marriage, who they will be with, regardless of their station in life is perhaps a huge leap for mankind. In the past, it could be said that women were viewed as possessions, or properties traded for financial reasons, or titles. I can truly say that I felt vulnerable in that era," Jewel said.

"I see your point."

"I have to say that the striking resemblance with Brock's eyes and the count's was too uncanny not to mention. I believe that in a previous life, he also wanted to possess me, as did the Count of Sussex. Does this seem real, or am I unnerved?"

"I cannot say for sure, but you may have a point. We can resume next session at ten Monday morning, if you feel up to it? Perhaps we can learn more about the soul's reincarnated reasons for which they would come back to different lifetimes to have new experiences."

"Most certainly. I would love to see where the next session takes me!" Jewel said, sounding excited at the prospect of yet another regression, taking her to some far off land in her past life.

Before leaving the restaurant, the professor asked, "Have you heard of any updates on the trial of Brock Simms and Officer Bill Casey?"

"I haven't heard back from Spence, though I hear there are complications with the others involved, especially with Mr. Michael McKay. I left Spence a message, but with his workload, I imagine he hadn't had the time to return my call," Jewel added.

Later while driving home, she wondered why the professor was so curious about this case. Perhaps it was the implications of the professor's assistant, Jamie Furrow that intrigued him.

The next week as arranged, they both resumed the session to carry Jewel away to another time in her spirit's life.

"Now are you prepared for this?" the professor asked, as Jewel lay down on the couch.

"Yes, of course."

"I want you to relax and take a deep breath." Jewel did as bidden. "That's good. Now you are getting quite sleepy and very relaxed…" He swung his watch back and forth. "That's it. Now you are totally calm, relaxing with no worries. You are at the top of the staircase. There are ten steps you must descend. And once you step down onto the last step, you shall find yourself back into time. Begin stepping down the first one and once I've counted down to ten, you will arrive at your next destination." The professor counted down to ten. "Where are you?"

"I'm not sure. It looks like a small town. Yes, I see the sign outside of town. It says Salem Massachusetts, that's where I am."

"Do you know who you are?"

"Yes, I'm Samantha!" Jewel repeated in a child's voice.

"That's good. What else do you see?" Professor Brown probed further.

"What do you mean...? My best friend Sarah is..." The words trailed off. Samantha could only watch in disbelief as the ten-year-old Sarah was marched up the steps of the gallows. What could she have done to warrant a hanging? Samantha looked around to see if she could recognize a single soul. Yes! There was Aunt Harriet. Why won't she stop this insanity? Samantha tried to yell out to her, but it was as though she couldn't get the words out, as if being in a nightmare. The words would not come out to save her life, not to mention Sarah's life too!

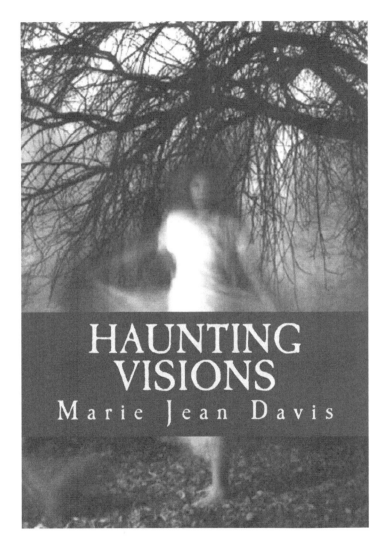

VOLUME 1

26129899R00147

Made in the USA
Middletown, DE
22 November 2015